"I thought you said Grandma invited all three of us,"

Jory said suspiciously. "What's a gauntlet, anyway?"

Larissa laughed while Matt looked at the floor. "It can be a heavy metal glove like knights wear. However, I suspect in this case it's kind of like an obstacle course filled with people who want to grab you. And your dad is right—I'm not ready to run the relative gauntlet with your grandmother yet. I'm only the hired help, not a marriage prospect."

"What's a prospect? Is it like panning for gold?"

Matt's lips were twitching. "Don't look at me," Larissa told him.

"A prospect?" Matt stalled. "Yeah, it's something like panning for gold. Except sometimes you come up with gold, and sometimes you get that gritty stuff from the bottom of the river that's like gravel, only nastier."

Larissa seriously considered pouring the rest of the coffee on Matt's head....

Dear Reader,

Take one married mom, add a surprise night of passion with her almost ex-husband, and what do you get? *Welcome Home, Daddy!* In Kristin Morgan's wonderful Romance, Rachel and Ross Murdock are now blessed with a baby on the way—and a second chance at marriage. That means Ross has only nine months to show his wife he's a FABULOUS FATHER!

Now take an any-minute-mom-to-be whose baby decides to make an appearance while she's snowbound at her handsome boss's cabin. What do you get? *An Unexpected Delivery* by Laurie Paige—a BUNDLES OF JOY book that will bring a big smile.

When one of THE BAKER BROOD hires a sexy detective to find her missing brother, she never expects to find herself walking down the aisle in Carla Cassidy's *An Impromptu Proposal.*

What's a single daddy to do when he falls for a woman with no memory? What if she's another man's wife—or another child's mother? Find out in Carol Grace's *The Rancher and the Lost Bride.*

Lynn Bulock's *And Mommy Makes Three* tells the tale of a little boy who wants a mom—and finds one in the "Story Lady" at the local library. Problem is, Dad isn't looking for a new Mrs.!

In Elizabeth Krueger's *Family Mine*, a very eligible bachelor returns to town, prepared to make an honest woman out of a single mother—but she has other ideas for him....

Finally, take six irresistible, emotional love stories by six terrific authors—and what do you get? Silhouette Romance—every month!

Enjoy every last one,

Melissa Senate
Senior Editor

Please address questions and book requests to:
Silhouette Reader Service
U.S.: 3010 Walden Ave., P.O. Box 1325, Buffalo, NY 14269
Canadian: P.O. Box 609, Fort Erie, Ont. L2A 5X3

AND MOMMY MAKES THREE

Lynn Bulock

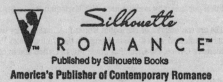

Silhouette
R O M A N C E™
Published by Silhouette Books
America's Publisher of Contemporary Romance

To Joe, always.
And to Mary, Debi and Debbie. They know why.

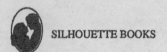 SILHOUETTE BOOKS

ISBN 0-373-19154-5

AND MOMMY MAKES THREE

Copyright © 1996 by Lynn M. Bulock

Books by Lynn Bulock

Silhouette Romance

Surprise Package #1053
And Mommy Makes Three #1154

LYNN BULOCK

lives near St. Louis, Missouri, with her husband and two sons, a dog and a cat. She has been telling stories since she could talk and writing them down since fourth grade. She is the author of nine contemporary romance novels.

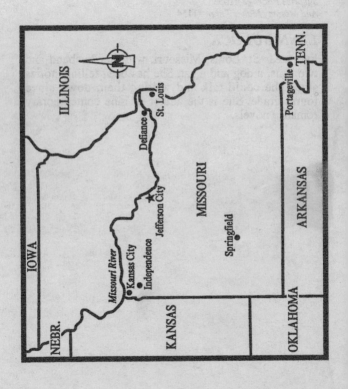

Chapter One

It was the voice that drew him first. Matt Viviano stood in the middle of Dardenne Library and listened to magic. He tried to resist, even while Jory was pulling at his hand with all the strength a six-year-old could muster. "Come on, Dad. I'm going to miss the story lady."

"All right." Matt didn't want to go anywhere there was a voice like that. A voice of husky timbre that sounded on the edge of laughing. A voice of smoky, seductive power.

"And this girl had an unusual name. Of course lots of folks back then had unusual names, like Jedediah and Methuselah and Hepsibah." There was laughter from the crowd of children and their parents clustered on the carpeted risers of the storytelling area of the library. Jory tugged his father down to sit on the riser in the back of the area.

He sat and continued to listen even as every bit of his common sense said he should flee. Sitting listening to this woman weave tales was dangerous. It brought back old feelings and memories he thought he'd drowned long ago.

He couldn't walk away. The voice wouldn't let him. It was seducing him before he even looked at the owner. Maybe if he didn't look he could leave. He'd go and read a magazine in the corner of the building farthest from here. Then he might be safe.

"This girl's name was Truelove," the voice continued. "Everybody called her that because she was the kindest, gentlest soul you ever wanted to see. She lived with her daddy down in the Ozark Mountains. Her momma had died a long time before, but she'd taught Truelove everything she knew about physicking people before she'd gone. Anybody know what physicking is?"

Healing, Matt said silently. Suddenly he knew what this story was, knew where it was going, and he was lost.

It was too late to turn back now. He might as well watch and listen as rapt as Jory, elbows resting on skinned and calloused knees, shock of dark blond hair falling over his thin face. He looked in the direction Jory was looking, to the storyteller.

If her voice had begun to seduce him, her face finished the job. She was tall and slender, probably too thin. Her hands were delicate, and wove patterns in the air like birds in flight to go along with her tale. Pale curls bounced around her pointed face. His grandmother would call it a cat's face.

Nonna told this story. Not the way this woman was telling it, but the old woman had told him this story in his boyhood. It was part of the spell she'd woven, his whole family had woven. The spell that convinced him that people were good, the world was a fine place to be, and he belonged in it. That was before he knew better.

The words flowed around him as he was transported back to a warm kitchen smelling of simmering tomato sauce and the sharpness of fresh grated cheese. His mother was getting dinner and Nonna was sitting in a rocker, telling him this story.

Except when she'd told it, the setting had been Florence and Venice and the fair Gilette was a physician, not a "physicker." But it was all here again, no matter what the woman called her heroine.

This heroine was just as brave and true as Nonna's. Her noble husband, saved by her skills and forced to marry her, was just as awful. And here she was trying to figure out how to do what he ordered and show up with his child in her arms and his ring on her finger. No, wait, there was a change after all.

"... leading my favorite horse by its halter, and wearing my ring on your finger. Then you'll be my Truelove," she said.

So, Matt thought, a revisionist. Not quite so magic after all. He'd have to talk to her after this was over and ask her about this stupid horse. It threw the story off.

Who was he fooling? He didn't want to ask this woman about a horse. He wanted to ask her to come home with him. To sit in his kitchen in a rocker and weave the magic his grandmother had woven. To make the big, empty barn of a place into a home. He wanted it so badly that he could feel his hands shake. And he didn't even know her name.

* * *

He was still watching her. This was silly, Larissa thought. She'd been at this too long to have someone watching her get her rattled. People were supposed to watch storytellers. But few of them past the age of four watched with this intensity.

He had a child's hunger for the story, Larissa thought as she tried to keep the story on track and not look at him. That was hard, when he was so compelling. Dark brown hair, a bit unruly, and bright eyes. Hazel, perhaps. He was too far away to be sure. It was good that he was in the last row. She could concentrate on folks farther down and not worry about those intense eyes on her.

There was a child next to him, a little boy. He was enthralled by the story and Larissa decided to tell it to him. That was easy; the little tanned, open face drank in her every word. The boy didn't have the same kind of scowl as his daddy. Her watcher had to be his daddy. There was too much similarity in the coloring of the pair, and the way they both leaned forward, stretching out long legs.

Larissa forced her concentration back to True-love. She could tell this story in her sleep. Surely she could tell it while one handsome stranger watched along with her normal library audience. Even after what had happened to her recently, she was a story-teller first and foremost. She could ignore this stranger and go on telling her tale.

Finally she was almost done. The noble young man had to admit that the girl had his best horse. And his ring. And she was standing in front of him. Larissa imagined that she had a smug little grin on her face for finally outsmarting him. Why did she love him so

much after all this mess he'd put her through? It
didn't matter. What mattered was the story and telling it.

"So he took her in his arms," she said, getting
ready to finish. "Then he kissed her. And he told her,
'Surely you're my own Truelove. And now I'll take
you home.' So they got up on his finest horse and
that's where they went. Home. And we best be getting there too." Then she stopped and there was a
satisfied hum to the audience before they started
clapping. The librarian bustled up and the crowd
started moving and her stranger faded into it. Without his gaze on her Larissa felt as if someone had
turned out a light.

There was a crowd of children around her and she
couldn't go look for one adult stranger. Not when she
was getting a raft of hugs and thank yous and one
little girl was telling her all about *her* horse and Larissa had to make interested noises.

Then the first wave of children was gone and the
boy she'd told the story to was in front of her. Up
close she could see that his eyes were hazel. And his
knees were skinned. And on his face was a slightly
hungry expression that made her want to smooth his
hair off his forehead. "My daddy says you made up
the horse," he said solemnly.

Larissa felt as if something viable had taken hold
of her shoulders and rocked her back on her heels.
"He's right. I did make up the horse."

"He says it's better the other way. The story, I
mean. Would you tell it to me? The way without the
horse?"

"Well, maybe sometime," Larissa hedged. It was hard to tell someone quite so solemn and forthright no.

"My grandma's fixing spaghetti for supper. Want to come home with me now and tell it?"

Now she really was stuck. "I don't think so. It's nice of you to ask, but most grown-ups have a rule about knowing the people they feed supper to."

"I know you already," the child insisted. "It's not like you're a stranger or something."

"But that's exactly what I am," Larissa said, knowing even as she said it that she hadn't been a stranger to this child since the moment she laid eyes on him.

"No, you're not. You're the story lady. Let me ask my dad."

He was gone before Larissa could protest. While he vanished she looked around for the canvas bag that held her things. Perhaps she could gather it and her purse and be gone before he came back for the awkward part after his father told him no.

The bag was easy, but she had no idea where Tess, the librarian, had put her purse. Probably behind that huge counter she called a desk over in the corner. It was besieged with children getting stickers for the summer reading program.

Larissa wedged her way through the mass of small bodies and looked under Tess's counter. There was her battered purse. As she slipped the strap on her shoulder, the boy was back.

"Tess says you're okay. Jory's invitation stands," the man next to him said. He was as solemn as the child and his eyes were the same shade of hazel.

"That's real nice, but I don't know you. And even if Tess would vouch for you as well as me, I'm not going to impose on total strangers," Larissa said.

Even as she said it she knew she wanted to go with him. To see what kind of home the man in the tan shirt had. To see how he knew she'd made up the horse. Every shred of her common sense told her she should head for the hills, but here she was still standing next to him.

"I'm Matt Viviano. Jory's dad," he said as if the last addition made everything all right. "And Tess will vouch for me. And my mother cooks like she's feeding the seventh fleet. There will be plenty of spaghetti, so you don't need to feel as if you're imposing."

"I'm Larissa Camden. Tess's houseguest, at least for the time being. Let me go talk to her."

Tess, in the middle of handing out stickers to the masses, looked at Larissa with sparkling eyes. "Yes, of anybody that was here today, if you're going to go home with somebody, go home with Matt. He's a conservation agent, he's lived here forever, and he has the one house in Defiance that didn't even have a wet basement in the flood. If he invited you for supper, you're welcome to go."

Larissa had planned to tell Tess why she wasn't going with the handsome stranger, but now she reconsidered. Tess and her family had been putting up with her night and day for two weeks. Surely they'd like a little bit of normal life back without company. She hadn't found a place of her own yet, and she knew virtually no one except Tess and the principal of the elementary school who'd hired her. Maybe she *would* go to Matt's for dinner.

No, she corrected herself, she'd go to *Jory's* for dinner. The child was the one she should concentrate on. He looked as if he could soak up love like rain. She winced inside, knowing that she was about to do it again. She was about to reach out to someone and cause herself a world of hurt. Someday she'd learn not to reach out.

But she hadn't learned yet, and Jory was still standing next to his father, one bare leg rubbing the other where several mosquito bites decorated his tan skin. "All right," she said, crossing the space between them. "Tell me how to get to this spaghetti dinner." She had to be out of her mind.

Pulling up to the house in his battered truck, Matt looked at it the way a stranger might. What had he been thinking at the library, telling Jory the story lady could come home for supper? Sure, his mom's spaghetti was the greatest. Even now the place would smell like heaven inside, the air heavy with basil.

But outside the lawn hadn't recovered from being underwater this summer, and the siding was weathered. It looked like exactly what it was, a big old barn of a house with a single owner too busy to keep it up.

When was the last time the windows had been washed? There was a bicycle on the front porch, leaning drunkenly against the house because it had no kickstand. He'd taken Jory's training wheels off, but never put the kickstand on the bike.

There were no curtains in the living room. The windows stared back at him as he got out of the truck. They looked dull and empty. The whole room was pretty empty once you went inside. No furniture in there at all anymore except his desk and a couple of plastic crates full of conservation pamphlets and books. Damn, what had he been thinking?

It had just been too tempting, he guessed. A beautiful woman whose hands wove magic. Dark gold eyes and a lilting voice, and her story, one that could touch his heart like no other. It had spoken to him in places he didn't know existed anymore and when Jory begged to take her home he'd agreed, as if she were some raccoon that had knocked over the trash instead of a dangerous, adult human being of the female persuasion.

Now she was pulling up into the driveway in her little yellow car. What sane human being drove a car that color? She bounced out of the car, not bothering to lock the door, and bounded over to the truck.

"Tess says you didn't get too wet in the flood. I'll bet you're glad. This house must be a hundred years old."

"Close to," Matt said, feeling shy and withdrawn again. "Come on in."

The house looked every bit of its age as he ushered her through the front hall. On the table there was a week's worth of mail, at least. Under it he could have written his name in the dust. Larissa didn't seem to notice.

"Oh, Jory," she crooned. "Your grandma makes wonderful spaghetti."

Jory wrinkled his nose. "How do you know? You haven't even tasted it."

"Yeah, but I can smell it," she said. "And she uses real herbs and plenty of them." She took another whiff, lifting her face as if to a spring shower in a gesture that made Matt's chest ache. "And wine too, I'll bet."

"I dunno. She just dumps stuff in and cooks it until it's done. In between she reads me a story. Want to come meet her?"

"Sure," Larissa said, letting the child take her down the hall into the kitchen at the back of the house while Matt watched. He took his hands out of his pockets, wondering if he'd been scowling while he watched them. The rest of his posture sure didn't speak of the perfect host—shoulders hunched, hands thrust deep into his pockets—and he'd let his guest and his son do all the talking. It seemed as if they both had plenty to say. Chances were good neither of them noticed his antisocial behavior. And Connie would just add to the jumble.

He looked at that huge stack of mail. Maybe he should sit at the desk and take care of it. If he was lucky Connie would give the woman his life's history while he browsed and she'd run screaming back to her little yellow car and he'd never have to worry about her again. He looked again. Even on his front table there probably wasn't that much mail. Still, it was worth a try.

After ten minutes with Connie Viviano, Larissa felt as if she'd been adopted. Matt's mother was a small woman, dark and birdlike. Her slenderness looked deceptively frail, but from her actions Larissa knew that small body might as well have been made out of steel cable. She had the same vigor about her as Aunt Stell had up until the day she died. Larissa knew from personal experience that it would take something of hurricane force to stop a woman like this.

Since there was no hurricane in the kitchen, she kept going. Connie made a triangle between stirring the pot of sauce simmering on the huge stove, topping off Larissa's iced tea glass with fresh cold tea and clucking over Jory as he tore lettuce for a salad.

In between she kept Larissa busy answering questions. In ten minutes Connie knew more about her than anyone in the St. Louis area did except Tess. "Fairview? Jordan, isn't that your school?"

"Sure, Grandma." He puffed with pride. "I get to go all day this year. First grade."

"Well, Ms. Camden here is going to be the librarian. Did you hear her say that?"

Jory's eyes widened. "At my school? Neat."

"I imagine I'll see you there," Larissa said.

"I know you will. I'm going to the library whenever they let me. I can already read by myself."

"And I bet you do a good job of it."

"He does." Connie held a handful of pasta as if weighing it. It seemed to be judged adequate and she put it in the pot of boiling water. Giving it a quick stir and looking in, she added another handful not quite as large.

Satisfied, she moved back to the table. "So you're living with your friend, the librarian at Dardenne. Is that a permanent arrangement?"

"Well, no. I didn't realize it would be so hard to get a place." The summer floods had been devastating and rental property was at a premium. Of course, so was her money. With her current situation it was going to be difficult, if not impossible, to come up with the first month, last month and deposit that most landlords wanted.

She hadn't realized that flight would be so expensive in so many ways. But it had drained her emotionally as well as draining her bank account. Larissa had been spending all her free time looking for an apartment she could afford, but so far nothing had turned up.

Connie cocked her head, looking more like a sparrow than before. "How good are you with kids? You cook? Need low rent?"

Larissa felt a little winded, but shot the answers back at her as quickly as Connie had fired the questions. "Kids are the reason I work in a grade school. And I cook well enough. And yes, I need a fairly cheap place." That much she could admit without looking like a fool. "Why?"

Jory looked between the two women. "Are you interviewing her, Grandma?"

"It's a possibility, Jordan."

"Dad'll have a cow."

"I doubt it. Besides, I need to get back home."

"But I thought you liked it out here with us, Grandma."

The older woman ruffled his hair. "I like you, Jory. In fact, I love you best of all my grandsons."

"I'm your only grandson," he said with a giggle.

"No matter. I love you. I do not love the raccoons in your trash can. And I do not love that fellow who suns himself in the backyard."

"Mr. Snake? Dad says he's an important part of the ecosystem. He eats bugs."

"Mice, too, but he gives me the willies. Besides, Jory, my bingo buddies miss me. And I miss walking to mass every morning. And you need someone younger than Grandma chasing after you."

Connie looked straight at Larissa. "My son is...well, he's single. A widower. And with his job he needs a housekeeper full-time for Jory. Daycare just doesn't cut it, even if Matt wasn't so picky. He's gone strange hours, out catching poachers on the river and whatever it is he does the rest of the time for the Conservation Department. I'm helping out right now, but he needs a full-time person.''

Larissa raised her hands, palms up. ''Can't be me. I've already got a full-time job.''

''Nonsense. You need a place to live. He needs somebody to live in. You're going to be at school the same hours as Jordan. Surely they let you leave once the kids go home?''

''Well, normally they do. As long as I had a computer here I could probably do almost everything outside of school hours. But really, Mrs. Viviano...''

''Connie.''

''Connie,'' Larissa said, feeling as if she were being relentlessly plowed over by one of those machines that flattened asphalt. ''I don't think this is a good idea.''

The small woman drew back. ''Is there something wrong? Jory is a wonderful boy.''

''I'm sure he is. But if his father is looking for a housekeeper, I'm sure he's looking for someone with credentials. Experience.''

Connie wouldn't be budged. ''You said you cook. And you need a place. And Jory wanted you to come home for dinner. He doesn't warm to strangers. Those are enough credentials for me.''

''I can't imagine they'd be enough for your son.'' Larissa had seen him so far as a demanding person. If Matt Viviano was looking for a housekeeper she'd have to be a domestic scientist.

"He isn't that much of an ogre." Connie stirred the pot on the stove.

"Mom, are you discussing my fine qualities again?" Matt said, coming through the doorway.

"No. I'm hiring you a housekeeper."

"Now, wait a minute." It was his dubious expression that made Larissa decide on the spot she wanted the job. Aunt Stell had always called her the world's most contrary soul. Maybe she was, but right now what she wanted most was to prove to this man that she wasn't the helpless drip he obviously saw.

"I can do it, Mr. Viviano. I've got a degree in early childhood education, and I've been on my own since I was nineteen. Surely if I've survived this long I can take care of one small boy." *And his father,* she added silently. "And I'm not afraid of snakes."

At first Larissa thought adding the last bit was going to lose things for her. Then Matt's serious expression melted into laughter that transformed his face. Suddenly he was not only handsome, but as boyish as Jory. Larissa wanted to hug him on the spot.

"Let's talk about this more over dinner," Matt said. "Mama's draining the pasta, and she will not let it get cold. Her rules about dinner are one of the reasons I'm looking for a new housekeeper."

Connie's answering look was priceless. "Brat," she scolded. "Don't undo everything I've just accomplished in here. And yes, let's eat while it's hot."

Afterward, watching Larissa drive away in her impossible yellow car, Matt stood on the front porch wondering at it all. His mother had done it again. Somehow she'd maneuvered him into something impossible, something that wouldn't work out at all. He was going to let a storyteller be his housekeeper. This beautiful, ethereal young woman was going to be washing his socks and packing Jory's lunches.

At least Jory seemed happy about everything. And she could start right away, which made Connie happy. "If she's living with Tess and the school district hired her, she can't be a convicted felon or anything," he said aloud to try to still his misgivings.

No, there didn't seem to be anything wrong with Larissa Camden. Still, he had the nagging suspicion that letting her into his life was going to be the most insane, painful thing he'd done in years. Maybe even since Dee. On that note he opened the screen door and went inside. Some things didn't even bear thinking about on a glorious late summer night, and one of them was Dee.

"You helping your grandma with the dishes, squirt?" he called in to Jory. Better start acting like a parent. Unlike relationships with the opposite sex, parenting he was good at. Better practice while Jory still gave him a chance.

Chapter Two

"Are you sure about this?" Tess asked Larissa for what had to be the twelfth time. "I mean, I never expected you to come home from dinner with an invitation to live with Matt Viviano."

"You make it sound risqué," Larissa said, continuing to pack her suitcase. "I am not going to be living with Matt Viviano. I'm going to be working for him. Besides, you said he was okay."

"Okay to eat dinner with. I didn't think you'd move right in after one plate of spaghetti."

"The man has a wonderful old house, with room enough for six or seven people to rattle around in it without ever coming in contact with one another. There's a whole little suite for the housekeeper." Larissa closed the suitcase and hefted it onto the growing pile on the bedroom floor. "Matt's mom showed me everything. I've got a bedroom, a living room where I can set up my computer—including a separate phone line I can use for my modem—my own bath and a closet bigger than my living room in Portageville."

"All right. Have it your way." Tess had that look Larissa suspected she got when someone brought back a picture book their Labrador had snacked on. "It's the perfect situation and you're not just doing it to get out from underfoot here."

Larissa turned to her friend. "Is that what you think? I'm not, really, Tess. You have been so generous to let me stay this long. And I've loved being with the girls. But this feels right."

"Oh, Larissa, you could make moving in with an ax murderer feel right."

Larissa felt a cold stripe move down her spine. "Is he? An ax murderer or something?" Suddenly all the confidence at her new decision was evaporating.

"Oh, no, honey. Not at all. But it's so fast," Tess said.

"I do almost everything fast. And it works most of the time," Larissa argued. Squarely between them, as solid as one of her suitcases, was the knowledge of the last time it hadn't worked out. The time that had resulted in her coming to live with Tess two weeks ago. But neither of them said anything.

Instead, Tess crossed the space between them and hugged her. "I'm sorry. I shouldn't mother you like I do the girls. You're an adult capable of making your own decisions. And even if this is a quick one, it's probably good. Just remember this room is going to stay vacant all summer if you need it, okay, Larissa?"

Her eyes misted over and Larissa hugged her friend back. "Okay. Now help me get all this stuff out to the car before I lose my nerve."

She kept her nerve through loading the car. It was still there during the scant few miles she had to go from Tess's subdivision to the hilly road that led toward Defiance. Before she crossed the main highway she stopped at a fast food place for coffee. No sense, she told herself, in showing up too early her first day at the Vivianos'.

That was a fib, she admitted as she finished her coffee. Connie had probably been up for hours, and Jory had without a doubt been waiting for her since dawn. She was losing her nerve. What if Tess was right? What if this was as poor a decision as the last one she made? She couldn't just keep leaving jobs and towns and places to live out of sheer embarrassment. This had to work out, at least for the bulk of the school year. And the school year was still two weeks from even starting.

Sighing, she put her nearly empty coffee container in the trash and walked out to her battered yellow car. Time to go face the music. In Matt Viviano's case, Larissa heard the strict tempo of a military march when she looked at him. "And here I am, a girl who likes waltzes," she murmured to no one in particular as she opened the door of the car.

When she pulled into the long rock driveway, Jory was out of the house before Larissa cut off the engine. "Grandma says I should help you carry stuff in. I'm pretty strong. I can take the heavy stuff," he told her, flexing his wiry arms for her approval.

"I'm sure you can. How about this one first?" Larissa handed the boy a duffel bag. He grasped it by both handles and hauled it toward the door.

"Grandma, she's here," he announced in loud tones from the porch. Still dragging the bag, he motioned to Larissa. "Come on and see where you're going to stay. I'll take this there and show you."

Larissa didn't point out to him that she already knew the way. He seemed so proud to be sharing his home with her that she wasn't going to burst his bubble. He got the door to her suite open and put the bag in the middle of her living room floor. "I helped Grandma wash the windows. And we picked those roses just for you."

There was a vase of bursting bright pink blossoms on an end table. "Oh, Jory, they're beautiful," she told him, unable to resist burying her face in the velvet petals. "Roses are my absolute favorite."

"Mine, too. They draw the most bees," Jory said. "But don't worry. We left the bees outside. Grandma said most people don't appreciate them like I do."

"She's right," came a voice from the doorway. "Ms. Camden will be happy to leave the stingers outside."

She turned to face Matt. He was even better looking than she remembered, framed in oak. He seemed to fill the opening, rumpled hair matching the stained wood and skin not much lighter from being outside.

"Mr. Viviano." Larissa got the feeling that even though Jory had left the bees outside, she'd already been stung. Matt looked even more uncomfortable than she felt. "Should I keep unloading?"

He seemed startled by her question. "Of course. In fact, I came to help."

"You don't have to, Dad. I'm already helping Larissa all by myself."

"How about calling her Ms. Camden, Jory? At school the other kids will be calling her that and we don't want to get into bad habits, do we?"

"I guess not." He slid out of the room past his father with a disappointed look on his face.

"I'll still help," Matt said.

"Fine. While you're helping carry in my computer, you can help Jory come up with another solution to his dilemma than calling me Ms. Camden at home," Larissa told him, watching his hazel eyes widen. "I'm not a very formal person. If you want me to call you Mr. Viviano all the time, I will. But I'd rather Jory called me Larissa. You, too, for that matter."

She wondered how her name would sound on his lips. The fact that it seemed to matter was a little disturbing, but Larissa pushed away the thought. She had to use her energy to get everything unpacked right now.

She was hooking up the computer, thankful that nothing had been damaged in her hasty packing and now unpacking it all, when a tawny head popped in the door. "How about Miss Larissa, like the lady at the library called you? Dad said it would be a good compromise."

"Dad's right," she told the smiling child. His grin was so contagious she wondered why his father wasn't habitually wearing one as well. How could anyone look at this little boy and not smile continually? Whatever kept the somber expression on Matt's face, it must be pretty powerful.

"Oh, yeah." Jory interrupted her thoughts. "Grandma says lunch will be ready in ten minutes, 'cause Dad's got to go in to work. That all right with you?"

"Peachy keen," she said, loving the giggles the goofy phrase got out of Jory. "I'll be there in two shakes of a lamb's tail." His giggle rang all the way down the hall to the kitchen. This, Larissa thought, was going to be an easy job after all.

It was going to be sheer torture, Matt decided. Everything the woman owned was fluffy and feminine and smelled of violets. There must have been ten boxes of books, or maybe they had been bricks. They were certainly that heavy, and each had that evocative scent he already thought of as Larissa's. She already had Jory eating out of her hand, not to mention Connie.

His attempt at formality and distance had fallen flat within ten minutes of her arrival. He needed all the space he could get between this enchanting creature and himself. Otherwise how could he keep remembering that he wanted to be single and unattached for the rest of his life? That he had no business getting involved with a woman? He wanted no part of any women or the heartache they brought with them, not even one as tempting as this one with her pretty feet tucked up under his kitchen table.

One look at his son struck down all his resolve to tell Larissa he'd made a mistake. If it wasn't for Jory he could toss her back out the door with her perfume and her stories and her magic. Of course he could. Jory was the reason for all of this in the first place. His job made it difficult to get in even the time he wanted to with the boy, and the schedule had driven most housekeepers nuts.

Larissa didn't look like the kind that would easily fluster, like that last one the agency had sent out. She'd lasted all of ten days and very little of her quick departure had to do with Jory and the garter snake, Matt was sure.

Jory didn't look as if he wanted to introduce Larissa to any garter snakes. His little face was turned to her like a sunflower soaking up whatever nonsense story she was dishing up along with lunch. But that was all right, Matt told himself. Jory needed all the attention he could get. As long as this woman lavished her attention on the boy and didn't get any funny ideas about *him* needing any of it, they'd be all right.

Matt's lunch, which had held scant appeal, lost the last of its attraction as Larissa rumpled Jory's hair. He could almost feel that caress on his own skin and it killed him to realize that he'd welcome it as much as Jory did. "I'll be late for work if I don't get going." He pushed back from the table.

"When should we look for you?" Her eyes were huge, rimmed with sooty lashes that made her look even more like a doe. If there was such a thing as a golden-eyed doe.

"I should be home about nine or so. I expect Jory will have been in bed a while by then."

"Oh, Dad." The whine was familiar.

"Dad's rules still hold even when he's not here, my friend," Larissa told him before Matt could start the lecture that sprang up. "Do you work this schedule all the time?"

"In the busy months, especially summer boating season, we have patrols on the river dawn to dusk. This week I'm working the 'to dusk' part." Now why was he being so careful in his explanation?

"Should I keep dinner warm?"

"No need." He had to get away from here. Nobody but his mother had kept dinner warm for him in years, and he wasn't about to let this woman start now. "Mom?"

His questioning look made Connie follow him out to the porch. "Thanks for everything," he told her, hugging her briefly. "Make sure Larissa has all the emergency numbers down pat before you leave, okay?"

"Fine, Matthew." Her eyes seemed to twinkle. "She's going to do just fine. Don't worry. And you're going to do just fine, too."

"About that, I worry," Matt said.

His mother nodded, a tiny smile still quirking a corner of her mouth. "But you don't need to. This one will stay more than ten days. I personally guarantee it."

That's what I'm afraid of, Matt said to himself. But he didn't voice his fears to his mother. Instead, he simply checked that all her bags were loaded into her car, then stowed his own gear into his truck and drove off, leaving her waving. Larissa's staying was far more scary than her taking off in a blaze of garter snakes. He'd take as many snakes as anyone wanted to hand him any day of the week rather than get involved with one beguiling woman.

Jory was scrubbed and in his pajamas. He looked smaller and more vulnerable that way, and Larissa wasn't surprised that he asked for a bedtime story. Of course, not one out of a book. "The story you told at the library. But this time without the horse."

"Will do," Larissa said. If Matt was the one who had pointed out to him in the first place that the horse didn't belong there, then he wasn't going to object if she told it the right way.

Jory made a great audience for a story. Those hazel eyes got wide at the right times, and he nodded well, but didn't talk and go off on tangents on her. Before she knew it, Larissa was sitting on his bed instead of in the chair next to it.

"Well, Truelove didn't mind leaving her daddy, not for this man. For anybody else she would have minded, but Storekeeper Jeff was special. And they made a happy home together there in the mountains. In fact, it was such a happy home that some folks were real jealous of their happiness. Sally Lou Hutchins was especially jealous because she always thought she would be the one to marry Storekeeper Jeff and have a piano that made music and real kid slippers that were soft on her feet. So one day when she was in the store, she told Jeff a story about Truelove. Except it wasn't true and it wasn't lovely."

Jory's eyelids were drooping a little but he wasn't fading all the way. Larissa smoothed down his hair while she kept on telling the story. It had the texture of raw silk. The feel made her wonder what his father's hair would feel like. She was getting the oddest sensation of being watched. As if there were someone besides just Jory listening to her story. It was almost like sitting at a campfire and feeling wild eyes on her back.

But that was impossible. The only other person who would be in this house was Matt. And surely he'd just walk right into Jory's room and come listen, or interrupt them to tell his son good-night or something.

But then, maybe he wouldn't. Larissa thought of his near-haunted expression when he'd left for work. Maybe he wouldn't just walk in. She pulled her whole attention back to Jory and the tale she was telling, trying to put away the feeling she was being watched.

"So, finally the day came when Truelove could do everything Storekeeper Jeff had told her she'd need to do before she could come back. She dressed the baby up in his best clothes, and she put the shiny ring on her finger. She walked down the main street of town to the store, and on the way when she saw Sally Lou Hutchins, she stuck her tongue out at her just for spite.

"The little bell above the store door rang when she opened the door. Jeff stood behind the counter like always when Truelove walked in. He was so surprised to see her that he dropped a bolt of his best dry goods. Truelove walked up to him, with Little Jeff in her arms and his ring on her finger and she said, 'Well, here I am.'

"Jeff looked at her hard, and then he smiled. 'There you are,' he said. 'With my ring on your finger, and a youngun that can't be anybody's but mine in your arms.' So he took her in his arms and then he kissed her. And he told her, 'Surely you're my own Truelove. And now I'll take you home.' So he locked up the store and they went home. Where we are already," she improvised, since usually that wasn't the way she ended the story. "Good night, Jordan."

"Night." He was pushed down into the covers now, fighting sleep as hard as a little boy could.

"Want me to send your daddy in to kiss you good-night?"

"Sure." He rubbed a hand across his eyes. "You going to? Kiss me good-night. I don't like kisses much, but I guess from you..."

"How about we stick to hugs? That way you don't have to compromise your no kiss policy." She hugged the bony little shoulders and turned out the light.

In the hall, outside the doorway, Matt stood just where she expected him. Nothing else could have given her the tingling sensation she'd had on the back of her neck.

"Thought you were there," she said, looking for reaction in Matt. She didn't get much. "Tell him good-night and I'll go put on your dinner."

"You kept it warm anyway?"

"Nope. We had cold sandwiches and a salad. That way I could give you the same stuff and still keep my promise." Larissa thought she'd been ingenuous, but Matt still scowled as he crossed the threshold into Jory's room.

His expression wasn't much more pleasant when he came into the kitchen a few minutes later. "You really don't have to do this. It isn't supposed to be part of the job."

"What if I like it?" Larissa challenged. "What if after eight hours of kid companionship I feel like an adult chat before I go put together the rest of my things?"

"Fine. But don't make a habit of waiting on me. I don't like it."

Matt growled like a bear. Larissa got the feeling that he liked it all too much and wasn't about to get accustomed to it. She got a quick flash of another woman, maybe even another kitchen, where there had been a light on no matter what time Matt came home, and something warm in the oven to feed him. For a moment she ached for him. Obviously he figured she was going to leave soon. Maybe that somebody else had. The whole feeling made her want to reach out and hug him the way she had Jory, but common sense kept her still. She just nodded and put his plate on the table. "Iced tea?"

"Sure." He'd washed up sometime, and the hair on his forearms glinted gold in the soft light of the kitchen. It looked as soft as Jory's and it was all Larissa could do to keep herself from reaching out to caress his arm when she set down his glass of tea. This was getting out of hand. She pulled up the kitchen chair farthest away from his and sat down, out of the way of temptation.

"So, what did you do today? You can already imagine what I did."

"From the looks of things, you got settled in, found your way around the kitchen and entertained my son plenty."

Had anyone ever been so appealing just biting into a sandwich? Larissa wondered.

"I had a pretty slow shift. Gave out a couple of limit warnings to fishermen, took one set of boaters in for drunk and disorderly on the river, but otherwise just cruised."

"Is there a lot of drinking? I'd think you'd have to be crazy to tie one on and try to run a boat down the Missouri."

"Then there are a lot of crazy people out there. Today none of them managed to kill themselves or anybody else on my stretch of river."

Matt went back to his sandwich and Larissa stopped trying to draw him out. He was tired and hungry. Let him concentrate on eating. Of course, that meant *she* concentrated on his eating too. And that could lead to trouble. Just watching that firm mouth too long was going to mean a cool shower before she unpacked boxes. No, better get up and get herself a glass of iced tea to keep her hands and her eyes busy.

She fixed it just right, dallying over the mint she'd pulled from the patch near the house before coming back to the table. Matt was more than half done with dinner when she got back, which was a relief. He still wasn't very talkative.

"You're not used to much company, are you?"

"Not really. I've been . . . alone so long. And usually the housekeepers keep to themselves. After a day of Jory, they need the rest."

"He's not bad. In fact, for somebody his age I'd say he was a stellar example of boyhood," Larissa said. "I haven't found anything crawling in the laundry and he has only one bandage on his whole body."

Matt's mouth twitched. It looked like a hard battle, but the smile finally won. "He is active."

"Extremely. But wouldn't you worry if he wasn't?"

"Probably. Keeping track of him does tend to wear out housekeepers, though. We've had six so far in less than three years."

Larissa waved a hand, trying to dismiss it all. "Hired the wrong people then. Not everybody likes the kind of housekeeping you've got to do with little boys around."

"You can say that again." Matt concentrated on the last of his sandwich. "But you do?"

Larissa didn't have to think about that question long. "I sure do."

His answering look was pointed. "Then how come you're just housekeeping? I mean, you're not exactly ancient, but if you like kids so much, why haven't you settled down to have some yourself?"

Larissa felt thunderstruck. Maybe this was just Matt's way of getting back at her for catching him in the darkened hallway, listening to her story. "It takes one component you'll notice I lack. A husband. And if they're all as nosy as you around here, you won't have to worry about my picking one up and moving out too soon." She dumped her ice in the sink, put her glass in the dishwasher and walked out without another word.

Leaving the room, she could feel Matt's eyes on her again. Fine. Let him watch her all he wanted as long as he was watching her retreating. She didn't have any more patience for his prickly personality tonight. The door to her suite was firmly closed and locked before Larissa unclenched both of her hands and took a sharp breath.

Before she got across the room to the boxes to take out her emotions on a storm of unpacking, there was a knock on the door. "Larissa?" Matt called softly.

She unlocked the door.

"I'm sorry," he said. "I'm really not used to company, I guess. I didn't have any call to say that. Please forgive me."

She opened the door wider. Matt looked truly repentant standing there and she couldn't be mean. "Forgiven. I'm a little sensitive right now myself. I shouldn't have reacted the way I did, no matter what you said. I guess for a while we're just going to have to move like porcupines on their honeymoon." Matt's confused grin made her explain. "Very, very carefully."

The grin spread into a lazy smile. "Yes. You're right."

She stepped back from the doorway. "Would you care to come in? I mean, it is your house."

He stayed in the doorway for a moment. "Outside this door it is. In there, it's all yours. I want Jory to respect that, so I should also. Nobody should be able to go in there without your invitation."

That was a comforting thought. After the last few months, with another person making himself comfortable using—and eventually taking—half of what belonged to her, it was nice to have her boundaries respected. But right now she was ready for company. "Come in, at least for a little while. I really do have to get back to unpacking."

"I've never known anyone with that many books," Matt said, motioning toward the boxes. "That or you have a rock collection of some scope."

Larissa laughed. "No, you were right the first time. Lots of folklore, lots of other stuff, and about a hundred yard sale finds and flea market bargains. I just can't pass up a good book."

He nodded. "With me it's chairs. You'll probably notice that there must be a dozen mismatched chairs around the house. I always think I'm going to get around to refinishing them and talking Mom into making matching covers. You'll also notice they are all still mismatched, in need of finishing, and upholstered in every color of the rainbow."

"So you'll have a busy retirement."

Matt shook his head. "Do you have an answer for everything?"

"I try."

Suddenly Matt crossed the space between them rapidly and put both hands on her shoulders. Before she could react to that, he kissed her.

It was not a long kiss, as kisses in her experience went. But there was more sensation packed into that brief brush against her lips than Larissa had dreamed possible. When Matt drew away she could only look up at him in puzzlement.

His voice when he spoke was uncommonly husky. "I just wanted to see if there was anything that you didn't have an answer for."

"Guess that's it," she managed to whisper before he fled, leaving her bemused and bewildered in the middle of the floor, touching a finger to her lips. She was speechless. That was a first, and it was thanks to Matt. She drifted off toward that cold shower. No books were going to get unpacked tonight.

Chapter Three

He had to have been out of his mind. Matt wiped the sweat off his face in the hot sun of the garden behind the house. Kissing Larissa had seemed such a good idea before he did it. And it had felt marvelous. And it had just the effect he had wanted of leaving her speechless. But since then he had had only one image in his mind: kissing her again. That was not what he had planned. He'd thought that kissing her once would have convinced him that was all he wanted.

Instead it had had the opposite effect. Since that brief kiss last night all he had thought about was his bewitching housekeeper. Bewitching was definitely the word for her. She was entangling him in a web of her stories, holding him in thrall in a net of pale hair and soft skin. And his response to all this was to kiss her, deepening the spell like nothing else could have. "Brilliant," he said, leaning on his hoe. He was probably the only man in history to bewitch himself with an unwilling witch.

She was probably in there now doing the dishes and humming to herself while Jory sat at the kitchen table coloring a picture. It sounded so homey and delicious. She was barefoot, in worn pale jeans and a tank top as a concession to the weather, that fluffy hair piled up somehow. Matt struck at the hard clay ground with his hoe, trying to banish the image from his mind.

Instead the image turned into the real, solid Larissa. "Thought you might need this." She held out a large plastic tumbler, beaded with moisture from the cool liquid inside. "You're working up quite a sweat."

That wasn't the half of it, Matt thought. Her tank top was white cotton with tiny little buttons down the front. He hoped feverishly that once school started she'd begin wearing outfits he remembered from the librarians of his youth. Suits of a severe cut. Plain dark dresses. Anything but the frills and cotton and worn denim Larissa seemed to favor. Then maybe she wouldn't distract him like that.

It wasn't so. Larissa would be distracting in a potato sack.

"Matt? You going to take this?" Looking puzzled, she was still holding out the cold drink she brought him.

"Oh, yeah. Thanks."

"We're out of sugar. Can Jory handle money successfully enough to go get me a bag?"

Larissa's question chilled Matt far more effectively than her drink. "He can count any amount of money you like. Inside the house. That child is far too young to go traipsing down the road to the store by himself.''

Her brow wrinkled and she was silent for a minute. ''I keep forgetting we're on the outskirts of a big city. Back down in Portageville that was the children's big entertainment, spending the change at the store. Okay, no walks to the store, at least alone. How about if I go with him?''

''Don't let him get out of your sight. Not for a moment.''

''Fine.'' Larissa turned away and started toward the house, then stopped a few feet away. ''Is there anything special I should know about Jory?''

''Other than the fact that he already reads at about a third-grade level and has been eyeing my radio as a vehicle for spare parts for science experiments?''

Larissa smiled. ''That explains his question about my electronics ownership. But yes, more than that. Is he prone to running away or something?''

''Not at all.'' The sweat running down Matt's sides had more to do with the conversation than with the hot August sun on his head.

''Then why am I playing Mama hawk? He's almost seven. If this lack of independence doesn't bother him now, it sure will soon.''

Matt stopped looking at her and went back to his hoeing. ''Then I guess we'll deal with that when it bothers him. Because the house rules stay.''

''Fine.'' There seemed to be a tightness to her muscles as Larissa turned away, especially in her back and her slim flanks in the worn jeans. It really seemed to aggravate her when she had to stop and turn around.

''One other question.''

"Shoot." Maybe he liked her even better slightly agitated. She seemed to crackle.

"How do I handle money around here? Sugar doesn't grow on trees, nor does anything else."

"There's a business-size envelope in the junk drawer."

"That one next to the silverware?"

"The very same. It has a hundred in cash in it, and I'll keep it full."

Larissa seemed to get even wider-eyed than usual. "And you give me a hard time for being trusting. Why not just put it in the cookie jar?"

"Nobody's taken any they haven't needed yet. If it makes you feel better, leave receipts on the counter-top for me, okay?"

She gave him a long, hard look. "Fine." Then she turned again and headed toward the house. And when he listened closely Matt could have sworn she muttered all the way. It was enough to make him forget sweating.

She was still muttering when she closed the kitchen door firmly behind herself. "Old mama hen, that's what he is. That little boy is too smart and too active to be cooped up with me all day." But she would keep Jory with her. After last night she was not about to invite more contact with Matt, and arguing with him just kept her facing him longer.

No one should look that good dripping with sweat and wearing dirty old work boots. But it wasn't the boots that had made her mouth go dry. It was the lack of other substantial attire on Matt that had made Larissa nearly drop his lemonade. He'd gone outside with a hat and a shirt to complement his jeans shorts. The hat was under a tree and the shirt hung from his back pocket, exposing a chest furred with chestnut hair. All of it just gave her another little mental snapshot to add to the collection that seemed to be displaying itself when she should be paying attention to other things.

"Store. We're walking to the store for sugar. Jory, do you have shoes on?" After that little exchange with Matt the child better be properly clothed. Not only shoes, Larissa figured, but a hat as well. Thank goodness he was too tan to need sunscreen or she'd have to slather that on him, too. Larissa caught herself in the middle of her mental tirade. She shouldn't be castigating the man for the simple act of wanting to protect his child. It was a different world out there than the one she had grown up in. Heck, she had the scars herself to prove that, even if they were all mental. If Jory wasn't allowed to walk to the store alone, she'd walk with him. They'd still have plenty of fun.

Larissa hoped that Jory wasn't allergic to bees. He had said he didn't think so, but he didn't ever remember being stung. The purple clover they were both sitting in would be the perfect thing to attract every bee in the county. But at least Jory knew how to weave a clover chain.

She wondered if anybody sprayed along these country roads. Hopefully not. She'd love to show him how to get the nectar out of these fat purple blossoms all around him. Just the smell seemed to be intoxicating him into giggles.

He was such a delightful child. Larissa had to restrain herself from ruffling his hair and dropping kisses on his nose. He was just old enough that his dignity probably wouldn't allow such behavior, especially from a female.

Right now his tongue was out in concentration, making a tiny edge of pink in the shades of tan on his face—tan hair flecked with gold, hazel eyes flecked with tan, freckles dusting across his nose in a slightly darker tan. Jory was a summer child. Larissa wondered if his father had those darker tan freckles she noticed on the boy. Getting close enough to Matt to discover the answer would be dangerous. It was safer just to watch Jory and wonder.

"Miss Larissa? How do you put this together?" He had a long clover chain, laden with blossoms, stretched between his hands. "I want to make a circle."

Larissa took the chain from him. "That is just fine and dandy, Jory. You are a champion clover-chain maker. I usually just tie a knot to join mine. Like a square knot. Know that one?"

"Not yet." He cocked his head and watched her while she tied the stems together. "You talk different."

"Thank you for not saying funny."

His dark golden face split into a grin. "Dad would kill me if I said anything like that to anybody. But you do talk different."

"Probably because I grew up someplace different, and the people who taught me to talk did, too."

"How far away did you grow up?"

"In real distance, less than two hundred miles. You could drive it in an afternoon. But in the difference between places, it might as well have been the moon, Jory."

She finished the ring of bright blossoms. "There. Now what do we do with it?" Handing it to the boy, she watched his face as he thought about what to do with his prize. She could tell the moment he decided from his satisfied smile, and felt like a woodland queen when he put the ring on her head like a coronet.

"Shall we make another one?"

"Sure. And you can tell me more about growing up on the moon," Jory said, his young-old smile telling her that he was teasing her and enjoying every minute of it.

Larissa was deep into her third clover chain when the voice interrupted her.

"You're going to get stung."

"Haven't yet. Today, anyway. Is Jory allergic to bees?"

Matt harrumphed. "Don't you think that was a question for before you plopped him down in the biggest clover patch for ten miles?"

"She asked me. I wasn't sure," Jory said defensively.

Larissa wondered what the two of them must look like to this stern figure who was now properly attired for work in his tan uniform instead of tempting denim shorts. Jory had one clover chain around his neck, and an anklet on his skinny right ankle just above his worn tennis shoe. Larissa was virtually upholstered in clover chains, decked in bracelets, a necklace, her circlet and one that wove around her like a Christmas garland. Feeling self conscious about how she looked in front of Matt, she almost didn't realize what his attire signified.

"Oh, brother. Lunch. I didn't fix anything yet, and you're ready for work." She tried scrambling to her feet.

"Don't put your hand down there. You'll squash a bee." Matt moved faster than she did, and scooped up both her hands in his, hauling her to her feet.

He did have those freckles, just like Jory. They were just a faint constellation across the bridge of his nose, burnished dots that barely stood out on his prominent tan. "But I didn't fix you lunch," she protested.

"Didn't expect you to." He seemed to have as much trouble as she did putting together coherent thoughts, and let go of her hands, stepping back. "Just as long as you fix Jory's. And yours. You strike me as the type of person who forgets to eat once in a while."

"Not often. Only when I'm really caught up in something important."

"Like making clover chains?"

"It's educational. Develops fine motor skills, teaches sequencing and provides a nature experience."

Matt looked rueful. "I'm sorry I said anything."

Jory couldn't wait for the adults to finish whatever conversation they were having. "Dad? We made you one. Want to put it on?" He held out his chain like a trophy and Larissa could see Matt's first impulse was to tell the child he was dressed for work and couldn't take his gift. Then a flash went through those hazel eyes that she could read from three feet away.

"Sure. Tie one on me," Matt said, holding out his wrist. He was a good daddy, Larissa decided, even if he was more strict than she would be. Underneath everything else there was a fierce love. The kind of love that let a grown man wear purple clover flowers to work to keep from disappointing a child. The sweetness in the air around her had little to do with the wealth of clover blossoms as Larissa watched the two, man and boy, walk back to the house together wreathed in purple flowers more precious than gemstones.

"Now, remember, you can't come in." Jory's voice was solemn as he let his father comb his hair. "You can drive me there today and you can park and we can walk up to the flagpole together, Dad. But you can't come in."

"And I can't hug you and I can't kiss you. Want a wave or a handshake?"

Jory seemed to be thinking hard. Throughout this exchange Larissa tried to look as if she were really doing dishes in the sink from the French toast and orange juice that no one really ate much of. Still, she managed to turn her head just right to see Matt, looking almost as well scrubbed and combed as Jory, fixing his son's hair before letting him go for this all-important first day of all-day school.

It tore at her heart a little. She'd never thought before quite how the parents must feel. She'd always been excited the first day to see how all the kids had grown over the summer, to see how tiny the new little ones looked and how much they seemed to mature in that first month as they got used to their surroundings.

But looking at Jory through a father's eyes, like the bright hazel ones that looked suspiciously sparkly, he looked so small and vulnerable. And determined to be his own person no matter what anybody wanted for him. Suddenly Matt's protectiveness didn't seem as out of line as it had for the last two weeks. He'd lost his wife somehow. Surely this little boy was the most precious person on earth for him. No matter that he hardly let him cross the street alone.

Jory finished his deliberation. "Handshake. And you can still hug me here, before we leave the house, I guess."

"Okay." Matt watched him leave the kitchen to finish getting ready on his own.

"Do you think it's this hard for everybody?"

Matt's question startled her a little. Larissa didn't think he'd admit to the pain he was feeling. He'd kept his feelings pretty much to himself for two weeks since that one kiss.

"I think it is," Larissa admitted. "But at least most families have two people to spread the worry between."

"This is true." Matt looked so serious.

"You do have a camera, don't you? His grandma will probably skin you alive if you don't take pictures the first day of school. Now that, I can testify, is allowable behavior at the flagpole."

"Then I'll make sure the film is still good. It's probably been in there since his birthday, if not Christmas." She watched Matt leave the kitchen as she pulled the plug on the dishwater and hung the towel. It had to be so hard, raising a child alone. She wondered again what had happened to Jory's mother. Whatever it had been, it must have been a while back. There was no trace of a woman's hand evident in this house except the curtains in Jory's room.

They had obviously been lovingly made by hand, long enough ago to be a nursery print that Larissa knew the first grader probably considered himself light-years too old for. But Jory was almost as sensitive and introspective as his father, and Larissa sensed that he wasn't going to tell Matt that the pale yellow walls of his room and curtains with dancing zoo animals were too young for him.

Maybe later in the fall when it was open-window weather she'd talk to Matt about painting. But not yet. Right now it was still so hot every day that the smell of drying paint would linger in the closed house. And right now Matt was having to let go of Jory's babyhood in so many other ways that Larissa knew it wouldn't be fair to heap one more on the burgeoning pile.

Her bag was already packed and ready by the door. She ducked into her apartment and made a quick assessment in the mirror. She'd pass. Satisfied she wouldn't scare the kindergartners, she headed for the front door.

"See you in the halls, Jory. And I'll stop by Mrs. Clemens's room to pick you up at three, okay?"

"Okay." The boy looked so excited he might levitate. It was catching, this first day excitement. Larissa knew she sparkled a little just from being near him. And Matt was almost as wiggly as his son.

"Well, come on. We need to get there, I guess. See you tonight about six?" Matt didn't even wait for her confirmation, but hustled Jory out the door. They were going to be so early, Larissa thought with a giggle. But then, so was half the first grade.

It was, in fact, more like three quarters of the first grade and kindergarten that were milling around the front of the school, Larissa thought, shading her face with one hand as she got out of the car. Matt at least was easy to spot. In the crowd of mostly shorter, female figures he was a rarity with his male height. A few other places there were daddies wielding cameras or shooting videos as part of a team, but Matt seemed to be the only lone male.

He was getting a lot of speculative looks. Larissa suddenly had a strong, irrational desire to join him and Jory, just to prove to any of those divorcées on the prowl that he was spoken for. *Spoken for?* She was working for him, for goodness' sake! That didn't mean a thing. No, best leave Matt and Jory to their goodbyes among any single ladies that might have kids around the flagpole. Larissa slipped in through the faculty entrance to the building and made her way to the cool, empty library. Maybe there the air-conditioning would ease the strain on her brain. Thoughts like this proved she had gotten too much sun this morning.

The library was where she needed to start her day anyway. There would be dozens of kids coming in sometime today for one thing or another and she had to be up to meeting them all. Still, it was hard to leave those thoughts of Matt out in the sunshine and focus on all those little tennis shoes that would soon be beating a path to her door.

By the time the door closed in the afternoon, Larissa was a little punchy with jubilation. She'd survived her first day on a new job. It wasn't much, but it would have to do. The first day of school for the year was always pretty wild, even in the library.

So far she'd met twelve of the "old" volunteers, signed up four moms with new first grade or kindergarten children, and gotten halfway familiar with the differences in circulation and filing on the shelves and in the computer system. It was much different from little bitty ol' Portageville. This school was huge and well stocked. Their books, most of them, looked brand-new and the computer was state of the art. She wasn't going to have to bring her terminal to school to serve as the main drive.

And down the second hall to the left, in among all the other tumult of everyone leaving for the first day, Jory was waiting for her. She wondered how his first day had gone. His teacher looked very nice from the few times she'd run into her in the halls the last week preparing for classes. And of course a stellar young man like Jory couldn't help but add to anyone's classroom.

Argh. She sounded like a mother instead of a housekeeper, Larissa told herself, wincing a little inside. But it was true. Jory was a gem. He'd take to first grade like a fish in deep water.

He was putting things in his book bag, concentration etched on his features, when she appeared in the doorway. "Jordan," Mrs. Clemens called. "Ms. Camden is here for you." He got up from his desk and headed for the door. "Hey, don't forget your deposit," his teacher said.

Larissa watched as Jory turned and went back to the slender young woman in navy slacks and gave her a hug. Her grin when she looked up at Larissa matched Jory's. "I make them give me five hugs the first week. That way I've always got one to give back to them if the going gets rough. Most of them like it so much they keep a running account.''

Their mutual smiles said more than words could, so Larissa just gathered Jory and left. Yes, he'd do fine here. If the bright pictures on the wall and the neat sentences on the blackboard hadn't told her that, his teacher's deposit account reassured her. It would be something to tell Matt at supper if Jory didn't.

Supper. Larissa sighed a little. Time to shift gears and go back to the second half of her job. "So, how was it?" she asked the boy striding beside her in the parking lot.

"Great. We have a hamster. Tomorrow we vote on naming him. I'm going to vote for Fuzzball because he's so fat he's round.''

So much for academics. Larissa smiled. Later they'd hear about that part of his day. Right now would be the important stuff, like hamsters.

"Hungry?"

"Starved. I guess I'm not used to eating lunch in fifteen minutes. But I know all the names of Billy Jenkins's brothers and sisters, and even his new cat.''

"So we'll stop for frozen yogurt on the way home, okay? Do you have homework?''

"Just easy stuff. I have to draw a picture of the best thing I did all summer.''

"Sounds pretty good to me." Larissa finally gave in to the temptation to ruffle the light brown hair.

"Yeah. I hope I have the right color crayon. Can I have sprinkles?''

"One scoop. Then we have to scoot home and do that homework. Deal?''

"Deal." She unlocked the car and Jory slid in. He looked light-years older than the child who'd left for school that morning. Larissa wondered how Matt would handle that.

By the time Matt got home, some of the newness had apparently worn off the first day of school. Larissa felt a twinge of pain that while she had gotten to see the classroom, the confusion and clutter, all he saw was Jory, on his knees in a kitchen chair working hard on a picture. He didn't bound out of the chair and at his dad at full tilt when Matt came into the kitchen.

"Smells good. What's for supper?" he asked tentatively.

"Spaghetti. Your mother left a casserole in the freezer just for tonight. I thought that was so sweet of her." Larissa willed the little boy in the chair to notice his father and start telling him all about his day.

The conversation at least stopped his drawing and he looked up. "Oh. Hi, Dad. I'm doing my homework." The head bent back over the drawing.

"So, you've got homework already?"

"Yeah. Not much. Mrs. Clemens says she's easy on us the first week."

"Tell me about that picture."

"It's the funnest thing I did this summer. Not funnest. That's not a word. Coolest, I guess."

Larissa looked over to the two of them, intent on the drawing. It seemed to feature a lot of brown, pink and green.

"See, that's you. And that's me. And that's my longest clover chain."

Larissa's throat closed as she was in the act of bending over the oven getting the casserole. The clover chain? That was the neatest thing he'd done all summer? She felt as if someone had just handed her diamonds. Still, she left Matt and the child to their discussion and kept being the housekeeper, putting the casserole on top of a trivet to cool down a little and going about the rest of supper preparation. But she knew that if anyone looked at her hard her eyes would be suspiciously glittery.

It was a good thing that Jory got loquacious over dinner and described everything about his day. It kept anyone from noticing that both the adults at the table were silent, passing each other dishes, pushing at food. Larissa knew why *she* felt edgy and tired but she wondered what was wrong with Matt.

After supper she had no time to ask. There was dinner to clean up from, Jory to get ready for the next day and settle in bed, and her own preparations for the next day to make as well.

It was long after dark when she caught up with Matt. He was out on the back porch, stretched out in a wooden chair with his feet propped up on the porch rail. Quiet, he seemed to be watching the fireflies glint in the dark beyond the garden.

"So? Should I pour us a glass of wine or something?" Larissa asked, sinking into the chair next to him.

"I don't think so." His voice was brittle and she longed to reach out to him. But she knew how that would be received so she kept her hands in her lap and watched him lean back, stretching out his long frame. "It's just another day, Larissa."

She felt stunned by his answer. "What do you mean, Matt?" This was an important day, a monumental one. Any father as concerned with his son as Matt was should realize that.

"I know what you're thinking. But see, they're all alike. Each day that Jory gets a little older, a little more independent, does something else major, it's just another day. Just another day that I do not have anyone to tell about it. That his mother didn't see. That fate, or life, or whatever, has managed to turn into just another reminder of how unfair life is to some of us.

"Deanna never saw him run. Never saw him draw a picture like that one he labored over tonight. Will never see him write his name in those firm letters he's so proud of. No, Larissa it's just another day."

The tears she'd held back in the kitchen were threatening so hard now that Larissa was thankful for the velvet darkness that swallowed them both up. Maybe in the dark Matt would also take the gesture that she couldn't hold back anymore. She reached out and found his callused hand and squeezed it once before she slipped out of her chair, left the porch and escaped into her room to think about the complex man still watching the darkness outside while he nursed an even darker place inside himself.

Standing in her room and brushing her hair with a fierceness that kept her from sobbing, Larissa coursed with emotion. It was hard to admit that she wanted to be a spark—Matt's spark—to light a candle in that dark place inside him so that he could find warmth and light again. Maybe the candle would gutter and go out. But even after she'd sworn she'd never care about a man again, Larissa wanted to care about this one. Because there was so much that was worth caring for in him.

But first he had to care himself and that, Larissa admitted, she couldn't make him do.

Chapter Four

The entire room smelled like apples. Larissa suspected that the whole house probably held a little of the perfume, but she hadn't been anywhere but the kitchen, so she couldn't say for sure. What she could say was that two windblown, smiling males greeted her that Friday when she came in the door.

"Guess I don't have to ask anybody how the orchard was." When she motioned toward the heaps of apples, Matt's smile was a little sheepish.

"Picking apples is fun. Kind of addictive, I guess."

Jory giggled. "Yeah. Dad says he's real glad nobody had to weigh him along with the apples when we left."

Larissa felt her smile join theirs. "Is anybody going to want dinner?"

"A late one. Small. And no apples, at least not tonight. But by tomorrow..."

"I get the idea," Larissa said. She put her book bag on the counter. "So, tell me all about it."

For fifteen minutes as she perched on a kitchen stool and ate one of the glowing Jonathans that sat in sacks on the counter, Larissa got a full account from Jory. She heard about baby pigs in the farm yard, the tractor-driven ride to the orchard, and their grand picnic once they'd picked apples.

Jory liked the cider press better than the cider. "It's just kind of squashy-looking apple juice," he confided. Obviously what he liked most of all was having his dad go along. His whole tale had been told while half lounging in his father's lap, half standing on the floor. Finally he ran out of breath and Matt ran out of patience for being a human jungle gym.

"Okay, squirmy. Go take a shower and change clothes in case any of those various weeds out there in the orchard were poison ivy. And how about starting on your homework so Miss Larissa and I don't have to nag you all weekend?"

"Okay." Jory slid off his comfortable perch and ambled away. There was silence as both adults watched him go.

"So, did you have as good a time as he did?"

"Better, maybe. Thanks for making me go."

Larissa looked up from her core. "I don't think I made you go."

"Not if you don't count leaving the permission slip with the 'we need volunteer parent helpers and drivers' part highlighted in kelly green on my desk, and casually mentioning to Jory that his old dad might have enough vacation days built up to go on school trips."

"Well, you did say that it was slowing down at work. And you know it's the one thing I can't do. They won't let me off to go to the orchard," Larissa said defensively.

"I know. And really, I enjoyed it. Those guys sure have energy. It's fun seeing things from their perspective. I don't think most of them had ever seen a baby pig."

"Or smelled one, either," Larissa said with a grin.

"Yeah, that was apparently a disappointment. However, things smelled so much like apples all the way back to school that everybody forgot."

"So, you weren't the only one to go overboard?"

"You should see the pile of sacks we left with Mrs. Clemens. But then, she says they're making apple something as a class project."

"Knowing Mary, they're making apple everything as a class project this next week," Larissa said. "I may steal some of her thunder and make applesauce tomorrow. Unless you really think we can do away with nearly three bushels just raw."

"Make sauce. Make anything. I think I need a shower, too." He stood up and stretched. "A long, hot one to take care of all the kinks caused by lifting twenty two first graders up to see the baby pigs. There are a few minuses to being the only daddy on a field trip."

Matt ambled out of the room much like Jory had and Larissa enjoyed watching him retreat. That long, lean male form was one of the definite benefits of being a housekeeper. And she was happy that convincing him to go on the field trip had worked so well. "Even if it means I'm up to my eyelashes in apples," she muttered to herself. "I've got to find a really good cookbook."

Dinner was indeed light and a little late. Jory almost nodded off in the tuna salad more than once. When he'd finished half a sandwich and most of his milk, Matt called a halt to the charade. "Okay, pal. Bedtime."

"'Kay. Long as Larissa tucks me in."

Matt was surprised. Even this tired he'd expected a fight.

"Will you?"

"Of course." Larissa rose from the table. "Leave all this stuff, okay? I'll get it when I'm done."

She looked as if she were asking him about more than just leaving the dirty dinner dishes, so Matt agreed. He got up, too, and hefted the unprotesting Jory up almost to his shoulder. It wouldn't be too much longer before he couldn't do this.

He could remember back to his own childhood, to that day when even his father couldn't carry him to bed when he fell asleep on the living room floor. Jory, with his colt legs and solid body, was getting close to that point. But not yet. Please, not yet. For a little while longer he wanted him small enough to have this incredibly heavy, sleepy head on his shoulder once in a while. It made him feel needed in a way he suspected he never would again once Jordan grew up just a little more.

They were at his room now and Jory curled comfortably under the covers. "You can stay if you want," he said to his father with the graciousness of a prince.

Larissa was already ensconced in the chair next to the bed, the bedside lamp turned as low as it would go. "Do I have to ask what you want?"

Jory's answering smile seemed to be answer enough. Matt stood in the doorway, watching her compose herself to tell the story. Her hands were wonderful. They were long-fingered, sure hands that he wished would forget themselves when they were alone together the way they forgot themselves when Larissa was telling a story.

Surely the flying motion those fingers made while she told about all of Truelove's escapades would be a wonderful motion to feel across his shoulder blades. It would be tentative at first, then stronger. She would discover the hunger in him that he kept so carefully hidden. And sometimes late at night like this, watching a nodding child and hearing Larissa's rich, husky voice, Matt wanted to share that hunger with her.

The rest of the time he knew it was foolish. He didn't need the pain of another woman in his life, not ever. Sure, Jory could use a mother instead of a housekeeper. But Jory's mother was dead. His son was going to have to face that problem and no amount of sweet bedtime stories would make it any easier.

Not in the long run, anyway. In the short run Jory was going limp into the pillows with a small smile on his face while Larissa had already reached the part about Truelove walking down the main street of town sticking her tongue out at Sally Lou Hutchins. Matt knew the story almost as well as Larissa at this point, and he still hated it.

It took him too many places he didn't want to go. That secure kitchen of his childhood. A high school hallway where he'd kissed Deanna. That shining college graduation before their wedding. All those places that had convinced him the world was a safe place where they would have this golden life together that lasted past the sunset.

Instead, it was dark outside now and he stood in Jory's doorway, watching the woman and child in their puddle of light and feeling like something feral watching a flickering campfire from the dark and cold of a ridge.

He couldn't bring the subject up right away when he and Larissa were finally settled in the family room for the evening. They'd taken to spending an hour or two together once Jory was down for the night.

In unspoken agreement, they talked very little in these nights. It worked out better that way. If they didn't talk much, there was nothing to spark the interest they both felt but wouldn't acknowledge. So they kept things safe.

Usually Larissa made a pot of coffee or tea, and sometimes she had a plate of homemade cookies out. She worked on library records from school, or some kind of handwork. It wasn't the same stuff his grandmother used to do. She'd worked with one slightly curved needle. This was with two that clicked. Matt had never paid enough attention to the fine details to know much more of the magic that appeared beneath either set of fingers.

Tonight Larissa seemed ready to start some new project. "All right, let's make you useful," she said, holding out a skein of yarn. Matt had no idea what she was talking about as she plumped herself down on the hassock in front of him. "Oh, come on. Hold out your hands so I can make a ball out of this."

"If you need it in a ball why don't you just buy it that way?"

"Doesn't come that way. And you're not doing anything anyway. Hold out those hands."

She was a little imperious in an impish way and Matt obeyed rather than argue. The yarn had an interesting texture in his hands, soft and heavy. Almost the way he expected her hair would feel under his hands if he finally wove his fingers through the pale mass.

Oh, damn. She stuck her tongue out the corner of her mouth when she concentrated. It was a trait that would have excited him in any woman. In Larissa it was spellbinding. It made her look even more feline than ever with her pointed chin and big dark gold eyes. That tiny pink tongue tip, just a shade darker rose than the lips next to it, peeked out as she wound the yarn into a ball. He could feel it whisper out of his hands, just like his chance to have a sane conversation was whispering away as he got caught up in the magic of watching her.

"Why do you keep telling it to him? That same story?" he finally blurted out. It lacked all the finesse he intended, but there was the question.

"It's the one I know best. I can tell it with no more effort than making this ball of yarn. Besides, he keeps asking for it," she replied simply. "It seems to touch something in him. So I tell it. That all right with you?"

"I don't know. It makes me uncomfortable."

"Didn't you have a favorite something when you were a kid?"

"Yeah. A story. That same story, but different. And I don't like what it did to me."

Larissa eyed him questioningly. "Did to you?"

"My grandmother told it. And other fairy tales. Nice, simple stories for nice simple people." Matt's voice sounded harsh even to him.

"We all need stories, Matt. It's not fair to raise a child without them. They need to hear the same words over and over. It convinces them that no matter how rocky the rest of life gets, some things stay the same."

"Yeah, well, that's garbage," he barked, still holding his hands stiff with the yarn. He watched as Larissa wound the last of it. It trickled away from his hands.

"For adults. But don't we owe children...oh, heck, don't we owe *Jory* the illusion that there are safe places to be and good people in them? Maybe if we work at it hard enough there actually will be for him."

"Sure. He's not even seven years old yet and he can't ever remember having a mother. His father works such screwy hours that he's never sure if he's going to eat breakfast with him or see him over milk and cookies at 9:00 p.m. Last year the river nearly ate his house. Yes, life is so full of safe places."

"Okay, so maybe I'm wrong." Larissa hadn't moved from the hassock and Matt was aware of the crackling aliveness of her just a foot away. "Maybe I'm living in a dream world. But I don't believe in teaching small children the harsher realities of life if they don't need to see them. Yes, people die. Nature provides floods and earthquakes and tornadoes. But we all need a safe place somewhere to call home."

"Where's yours, Larissa? In that town down south you left in such a hurry this summer?" Matt regretted the challenge he'd thrown down almost as soon as it left his lips, but there was no taking it back. He could see Larissa draw into herself, holding the ball of yarn tightly as her slender fingers whitened.

"Maybe not. And maybe you're right. Maybe I should stick to stories about little red steam shovels and train engines and things. Inanimate objects without safe places or caring hearts." And then she was gone. Off the hassock, out of the room, leaving Matt to feel once again as if he were at the edge of the fire. But without Larissa the warmth was fading fast.

The smell of cinnamon had taken over the scent of apples. Larissa wiped away at the damp little tendrils of loose hair around her face, trying to rid them of the moisture that clung to everything in the kitchen.

"This tastes really good," Jory crowed from the table. He was playing with a coffee cup full of warm applesauce, swirling it around with his spoon and then eating it in rosy dribbles.

"I think it tastes the best warm. It's sweeter that way." Larissa hadn't tasted it yet, hadn't experienced that warm velvety sweetness because she was afraid it would make her cry.

It would be difficult, if not impossible, to explain to Jory why the taste of warm applesauce would bring tears to her eyes. But it would. In a heartbeat that flavor on her tongue would bring back the old kitchen with its cracked linoleum. A big pan of Lodi apples and peelings, and a scarred wooden table with the conical colander and the wooden pestle that went inside where a little girl had knelt on a kitchen chair to squash apples through the sieve.

Aunt Stell had done the peeling, and the standing over the stove and stirring. Breaking up the chunks of steamy cooked apples had been Larissa's job. Then

Stell would take each panful, taste a tiny puckery bit of the summer green apples and add just the right amount of sugar. "It takes less if you sugar it warm," Larissa could hear her saying. Larissa always got packed off to sit under the big hackberry in the backyard with a cupful of the first batch.

Stell must have done quite a bit of work on those hot summer days while Larissa had been outside savoring that bit of sweetness made even sweeter by her work. Just one taste would bring it all back, she knew, the work and the worry and the love of that older woman who'd raised her when no one else had chosen to. She'd loved her and clucked over her until the day she'd died and Larissa knew the sweetness of one taste of applesauce would bring back all the memories, sweet and tart together.

She must have been standing in Matt's kitchen, remembering, for quite a little while. At least her hands had been busy while her mind wandered. The whole batch of applesauce was packed in freezer cartons, except for the bowl they'd saved to have with supper when Matt came home. Jory had finished his cup and left it on the table with the spoon beside it. She didn't even call him back to clean up his mess, as his father would have insisted and she usually agreed. Instead, she stowed the applesauce in the freezer and ran hot soapy water in the sink to wash up the table, the dishes and the general sticky aftermath of cooking with a small child.

"Stell, what would you think of all this?" she said to the spirit she felt hovering in the scent of spices. What would she think of the dark, silent man who employed her great-niece? Certainly somewhere she was probably grinning over Larissa wiping up the same sticky applesauce fingerprints she had herself twenty years before.

Larissa wished she had someone as insightful as Stell to talk to. Someone she could sigh about Matt to, maybe even find an idea about how to get under that rhino hide of his. Even if they never went further than just the cordial relations of a housekeeper and employer... No, who was she kidding? She let out the cooling dishwater. Certainly she couldn't fool herself into believing that.

She wanted to pour out her heart to someone. To tell someone who would understand about how much she'd come to care for the lean, silent soul who inhabited the same house as she did, but was never *there* with her. She wanted to find a way to make those wounded hazel eyes sparkle with laughter. She wanted him to kiss her the way he had that once.

The phone rang and she answered it absently. "Viviano residence. May I help you?"

"My, don't we sound professional," Tess drawled. "What are you and Jory doing?"

"Getting ready to go someplace with you, I hope. Do the girls like homemade applesauce?" Larissa was reaching for the freezer even before she knew the answer to the question.

It looked too dark to be six o'clock by the time Larissa was driving home. "Dad's going to be worried," Jory warned from the passenger seat of the little yellow car. He looked worried himself as he glanced out the window.

"Oh, we'll probably beat him home," Larissa said with more cheerfulness than she felt. The clouds were gathering around them and once in a while a low rumble of thunder sounded in the distance. Each new burst seemed to make Jory more anxious.

To tell the truth it made her more anxious too, but only because of what she was afraid they would find at home. If Matt had gotten there first, to an empty house without even a note to tell him where they had gone, Larissa could only imagine what he'd be like.

"We should have left him a note." Jory echoed her thoughts.

"He's not supposed to be home until at least six, sugar. We're going to be okay, you'll see."

It was about 6:15 when they pulled in the driveway. Larissa was annoyed to see Matt's truck already there before her. The storm broke overhead as they got out of the car and they both raced for the porch, reaching it just as the front door banged open.

"Where the devil have you been? Don't you know it's storming out?"

"Of course. That's why we were running." Larissa pushed her wet hair away from her forehead. Matt's distress seemed out of proportion for someone whose family was a few minutes late.

"Don't you believe in letting people know where you are? You're in charge here when I'm gone, Larissa. I don't expect to come home to an empty dark house and no idea where my son is."

"We were in the park with Tess and the girls. I didn't realize it had gotten this late, or the weather had gotten rough. We were so involved with playing with the kids that we didn't look up. Once I did, we came home."

Matt was still glowering and no one had gone inside. Just a few feet away it was pouring and the lightning flashed in the distance.

"I wanna go inside now." Jory's call was close to a wail. "I don't like this storm."

Larissa suspected he disliked the storm brewing between the grown-ups in his life as much as the real one spewing rain and thunder. "Okay, sugar." She turned to Matt. "You and I can continue this discussion later, all right?"

"Fine." His look told her it would be just as heated whenever they had it.

Inside, Jory showed no signs of calming down. "Is it going to storm all night? Will the river come up to the backyard again?"

"No, I don't think so. Why don't you get Flat Cat and we'll sit for a while together, okay? Bring that book about bugs from the library."

The disreputable stuffed animal and the book appeared in quick order and Larissa took boy, book and lovey into her lap in the rocker in the family room. Matt glowered but didn't continue arguing. Jory was tense and trembling a little, seeming near tears. They read about bugs until a particularly close boom of thunder made him shudder and clap his hands over his ears.

"I don't want bugs. I want your story. Please, Larissa."

"Let's keep on with the six leggity guys, Jory," she coaxed. "You could do a book report on this for Mrs. Clemens if we keep on."

Another burst of thunder brought an out-and-out wail and some tears from Jory. He was buried into her shoulder now.

"Forget what I said last night." Matt's voice was soft but still held a note of harshness. He didn't stay in the room to hear her start.

"Once way up in the mountains, in the hills of the Ozarks there was a girl with an unusual name. Of course, most everybody had strange names back then, names like Jedidiah and Methuselah and..."

"Hepsibah," Jory prompted. He was relaxing already, clutching Flat Cat and curling up in her lap comfortably.

"Hepsibah," she went on, repeating the words that were now as familiar to them both as old friends. Around the corner in the living room she could see Matt at his desk. If only the words could charm him out of his thundercloud, too. But no words Larissa could say were going to avert the storm that she knew was waiting inside Matt.

Finally the story was over. Jory had dozed off during the last part but Larissa had finished anyway, needing the practice for an upcoming storytellers' meet she was going to. Besides, she liked the heavy warmth of him in her lap. She knew that whatever excuse she used, she was just stalling.

Finally she couldn't sit with the heavy child on her lap any longer. She stood up with him and settled him, never more than half-awake, on the sofa. It wasn't storming anymore, just raining. She had slipped off her shoes while she was in the rocker to get away from having wet feet and now she padded into the front room barefoot.

That was probably a mistake. Matt had more height advantage when she didn't have her shoes on. He stood, pulled to full height once she came in. "Well?"

"He's asleep and all calmed down. In on the couch if you want to look."

His look was sharp and questioning. "Aren't you at least going to apologize?"

"I already told you why we were late. If anybody ought to apologize, it's you. You're the one who went nuts out there on the porch."

"Went nuts? You call genuine concern over a sloppily managed situation going nuts? Lady, you should see me when I really get upset." He ran a hand through already rumpled hair.

"I have no desire to, thank you. If you're going to fire me, do it and get it over with so I can pack."

"Fire you? That hadn't entered my mind. But it might be a good idea if this is your way of managing crises."

"What crisis?" She got close enough now to point a finger in his chest. "We were outside. We came home late. It rained on us. Is that a crisis?"

"It is when I don't have a clue whether you're in the park getting wet, which by the way is a lousy idea with all the big trees out there. Do you have any idea how many people die of lightning strikes in this state every year?" He was pacing away from her now, and wheeled back. "That's beside the point, anyway. What I'm trying to make clear to you is I want to know where you are all the time. If you go for a walk down the road, even, leave a note."

"I didn't think we were allowed to walk down the road. No sidewalks," Larissa countered. The look Matt turned on her was close to a snarl. He crossed the distance between them in a split second, his hands gripping her shoulders. "Don't make a mockery of my concern."

Larissa was stunned by the intensity of his feelings. "I didn't mean to. I'm sorry." He still hadn't relaxed his grip on her. "I think we're both a little overwrought here. And you have a valid point. Next time I'll leave a note. Fair enough?"

His hands eased up, but didn't release her. "I guess so. I was really worried, Larissa."

Even after he let go of her and walked away, leaving her in the unlit living room, Larissa continued to stand where she was for some moments. Because it wasn't the intensity with which he had held her that made her stop cold. It was his admission that he had been as concerned as he was—and not just for Jory. The look in those green-brown eyes had told her more than she'd wanted to know. Matt had been worried about both of them. She didn't know whether that admission scared her or Matt more.

Chapter Five

"Now, let me get this straight. You've never been to the Hill."

Larissa looked at Matt over the breakfast table. She seemed to be a source of amusement to him, and to Jory this morning. "I'm a country girl. I've been to lots of hills. But none of them were ever *the* Hill before. Enlighten me."

"Oh, you know. The Hill."

"Lasagna," Jory piped up. "Ladies who give me cookies. The neat church."

Now she was really more in the dark than ever. "I'm really clueless here. This place seems to be connected with Italian stuff somehow. And it must be a nice place if they give you cookies. But I honestly don't know what you're talking about."

Matt looked up at the ceiling. Larissa knew he couldn't be studying the cobwebs because since she'd gotten onto a regular cleaning schedule in the past few weeks, there weren't any. "Okay. The Hill. It's the Italian section of St. Louis, has been for generations. It's full of houses with narrow yards full of geraniums and birdbaths, small taverns where people play boccie and stickball, lots of shops of all kinds, and the cleanest sidewalks in three counties."

"Sounds pretty good to me. And you want to go there this morning?"

"Or this afternoon if it suits you better. I thought I'd even offer to take you to lunch."

Now Larissa felt a little suspicious. "Is this a date?"

Matt did his best not to snort. "Let's see. We're taking Jory along and we'll be in and out of about a dozen places getting the makings for a massive pan of lasagna and doing a little other shopping on the side. Does this sound romantic to you?"

"Okay, I get your point." It might have been nice if it had been an invitation to something more exciting, Larissa reflected. They'd called an unspoken truce the last two weeks and stayed to the general business of running the house, getting Jory places and sharing an occasional evening in the family room with a lot of classical music on the radio and very little conversation. But since the thunderstorm, nothing had been said about feelings, which appeared to suit everyone just fine.

At least it suited Matt just fine. Larissa was beginning to admit to herself that a truce with Matt wasn't what she wanted. Even if it was going to be a pain to further any relationship with him, it was going to be worth it. There was a man here definitely worth caring about. The longer she was around him, and his son, the more she knew that. But now they were waiting for an answer. Both of them had that extremely male look that told her she'd been thinking long enough.

"I can be ready to leave by ten-thirty," Larissa said, surveying the kitchen. Even having Jory help her make pancakes this morning hadn't upset things too much. "Should I change clothes?"

Jory was the one to look her up and down. "Maybe take a sweater. Otherwise I'd say she was okay, don't you think, Dad?"

Dad took the matter under consideration. "Pretty good, Jory. Now, how about going up to your room and making sure you're ready to go, too? Comb your hair—"

"Brush my teeth, find a shirt that buttons," Jory continued, not quite sighing. "I guess it's worth it. Does this mean Grandma is coming to make the lasagna?"

"No, I am. But I'm using her recipe. That okay?"

The look of consideration Jory gave his dad was so adult Larissa had to suppress a laugh. "It'll do. Don't forget the cheese."

Matt turned to Larissa once they heard Jory on the stairs. "Can you believe him? 'Don't forget the cheese.'"

"So, you're not always superdad. He still thinks you're pretty cool."

"That he does. How about you?"

His question unbalanced Larissa. What did she reply to a bald query like that? She could lie, but those hazel eyes would spot her falsehood in a minute. "Uh, I guess I think you're pretty cool too, Matt."

The smile on his face evaporated in confusion. "No, that's not what I meant. I was asking what he thought about you at school when you're just the librarian instead of his live-in buddy."

"Oh." Now she really felt like an idiot. "Well. I guess I have some status there, too. He hasn't gotten any check marks yet for rowdiness in the library, and he's gotten a pencil already. That's what you get when all your books for the month get turned in. Of course, when you're in first grade that's just two books in a month so it's not a challenge for a paragon like Jory."

"So you pass inspection at school, too?"

"I seem to." Before he could continue the conversation, Larissa started clearing the table. The syrup and the butter were back in the refrigerator and the scraps down the garbage disposal before Matt got up and drained the last of the coffee from the pot into his cup.

The action put him right next to her where she was loading the dishwasher. Larissa was conscious of his corduroy shirt nearly brushing her arm and the freshly showered scent of him.

"You really think that? That I'm pretty cool?" His shy smile was a little teasing but Larissa could tell he wanted an answer.

"A cool and dangerous customer, Matt. Why do you think I'm so far along with my knitting project? I have to find some way to keep my hands busy." It was fun seeing the color rise in his face. In one minute he had gulped his coffee and left the kitchen, muttering something about shaving before they went shopping. Larissa didn't even bother pointing out that he'd already accomplished that task. The poor man was rattled enough already. Why get him even more discombobulated, even if it was the truth?

For both statements were the truth. That perfect firm chin was already baby smooth this morning. And Matt was dangerous, at least where she was concerned. She'd never knit this much in her life and it was all just to keep her hands from tangling in that luxurious dark chestnut hair. Larissa actually whistled as she finished cleaning the kitchen.

She was like a child in delight. Matt watched Larissa swirling down familiar streets and saw them again in a way he hadn't in years. Not since Jory was in a stroller, reaching out to all the old ladies and their shopping bags, had he seen this neighborhood this way.

Since she wasn't a city girl, everything was different. She liked the dumb pigeons that strutted down the sidewalk. She was enchanted by the taverns where the perfect green lawns sported boccie balls. And Matt thought they would spend the entire morning in the bakery while she looked at the different kinds of cookies.

It would have been annoying except that the whole shop got caught up in watching and educating Larissa. The matron behind the counter, the one with the iron gray hair and stern disposition, got the giggles trying to make the Italian names for all the confections roll off Larissa's southern Missouri tongue. Heck, she even got samples.

In the end they'd walked out with two loaves of bread and a whole pound of delicate little cookies that they didn't need, but would be great with the wine he knew she'd get suckered into at the grocery. Watching her looking in the windows, speculating on prices with Jory at the furniture store, exclaiming over the tricolored fire hydrants, Matt nearly moaned. The grocery was going to cost him a fortune.

They got to the door and Larissa went right in and got a cart, surveying the narrow aisles in wonder. "Am I going to recognize anything in here? It smells wonderful, whether I do or not."

"I know it smells good. And yes, a lot of stuff will look familiar. And here is our list." Matt handed her the neat piece of paper. "We can buy what is on it. If it's not on the list, we aren't buying it. *Capisce?*"

"That means understand. Grandma taught me that one," Jory piped up.

"Okay. Then I *capisce*. I guess. Is it okay if I ask questions?"

"How could I keep you from doing anything but?" It would be annoying if it was anybody else, but with Larissa she was just turning his shopping trip into a party.

An hour later she was still in the grocery. Matt wasn't sure what enchanted her more—the strange shapes of all the different pastas or the names. "Oh, come on, Jory. I know it looks like one and you know it looks like one, but nobody would model a noodle after a belly button." With her hands on her hips she almost looked stern.

"C'mon, Dad. Help me out on this one." Jory looked up at him, urging him to solve his dilemma.

Matt had tried to stay out of all this so far. But this was too good to pass up. Larissa teased him senseless half the time. It was time to get back at her, just once. After all, they were in public. What could she do to him?

"He's not putting you on. It's the story they tell about tortellini." Matt picked up a package. "I mean, look at them. What else could possibly have this perfect shape? Round, indented, just begging you to put a finger…"

She was actually blushing. It was charming and made him want to laugh. Matt could feel his mouth twitching while he watched Larissa squirm. Why hadn't he realized before how much fun teasing her could be? She put down the package she was surveying down as if it were too hot. "Well, all right."

"Hey, don't go away yet. I was going to let each of you pick out a package of something, even if it wasn't on the list."

Jory didn't need any urging, reaching straight for the fusilli. "You should see what happens when you try to slurp these things. Grandma about had a cow the last time I tried."

"And what are those?" Larissa asked Matt. "If the other things are navels, what possible definition could those springy things get?"

"Why, you're right on the mark. Springs. Bedsprings, maybe? The way they're all tightly coiled and then you sit on the edge of the bed, and everything springs just a little tighter?" Their conversation was in low voices while they watched Jory race farther down the aisle.

This close to Larissa's ear, Matt could feel the wispy springs of her hair around his lips. What would she do if he leaned just a little closer and blew a soft breath down the open collar of her shirt?

He blew. She shivered. "I think we need to finish shopping and go outside in the nice, brisk fall air. Don't you?" she said a bit too brightly.

"In a little while. We still need wine. And cheese. Even Jory said we couldn't forget the cheese. And maybe some kind of sauce to go with those...bedsprings. What are you choosing, Larissa?"

By now she'd turned her face toward him and her expression had gone from discomfort to warmth. Her golden eyes sparkled. "I suspect your mother would indeed, as Jory says, have a cow if you brought canned pasta sauce into your home. The tomatoes still haven't gotten frostbitten or anything. He and I can work on something from the garden. I might even buy a package of these belly-button-shaped things, if folks will eat them."

"We'll eat them. You ever known a true Italian who wouldn't eat pasta in any form?"

"I've never known a true Italian before. And until this afternoon I wasn't so sure about you either, Viviano. I mean, the name fit. But you look so downright American."

"Not everybody who came from Italy was black haired, brown eyed and named Giuseppe, you know. I've seen people from the north who were as blond and blue-eyed as Swedes."

"Have you ever been there? Italy, I mean?"

It was Matt's turn to get uncomfortable now. "No. Dee and I...we always said for a second honeymoon. But there wasn't... We didn't."

Her expression got solemn in an instant. "I'm sorry. I didn't mean to make you uncomfortable. Especially when you're taking pains to show me such wonderful places. Let's go get the cheese."

Matt watched her course down the aisle and find Jory, who was pointing out the frozen squid. A bakery. Grocery shelves. This was what she considered wonderful places? The funny thing was, he was happy to know that these places were wonderful for Larissa, because they were just the places he'd want to share with anyone who was going to mean something to him.

He took a number at the cheese counter. That was silly. No one else was ever going to mean something to him again. Not when just the mention of a trip to Italy could plummet his feelings like this. Deanna had been gone for longer than they'd been married. It was time to get back to concentrating on the basics of life. No belly-button pasta. No pale-haired witches who made seed cookies into golden magic. No honeymoons of any number. Just a pound of mozzarella and some good Romano.

Back at the house Larissa looked around at the bags overtaking the kitchen. "Did we go a little nuts down there, or what?"

"Maybe a little," Matt admitted. "But it will all get eaten. We just have to find a place for it all until then. Not all, I guess. There's about a bag of stuff that goes into Mom's lasagna."

"You do have a recipe, don't you?" Larissa asked.

"Not only have a recipe, but intend to use it. You don't think I'd let a greenhorn like you be responsible for something as serious as lasagna, do you?"

"I didn't know. So if you're cooking, what should I do?"

"I don't know. Take a bubble bath. Eat bonbons. Whatever it is you women do when you have leisure time." Larissa would have hit him with a loaf of Italian bread if he hadn't been grinning so broadly.

"I'll keep myself busy, Matt. See if I don't." It was fun seeing the little look of worry cross his face that way. Maybe it almost got him back for that belly-button stuff in the grocery store.

By the time Larissa was done with her project she almost needed the bubble bath. In fact, she decided, putting in the last stake on the tent, she was going to take one. And then she was going to slip into clean clothes and find some candles. Might as well do this up all the way.

On the way into the house she detoured into the kitchen. "This smells fabulous," she told the two to-mato-sauce-spattered males in the room.

"Yeah, well, it better," Matt muttered. "Darn recipe takes every bowl and pot in the kitchen. Which I will clean up," he added. "I wouldn't sic this on anybody else. What have you been doing in the garage and the attic and everywhere else I've been hearing the patter of little feet?"

Jory giggled at the use of the term. "Oh, Dad. It was just Larissa. Do you really think her feet are that little?"

"Smaller than mine."

Larissa decided he looked good with that little bit of sauce on his cheekbone. It was probably evil to wonder how it would taste. Perhaps she needed a cool shower more than a warm bubble bath.

She took the bubble bath anyway, luxuriating in it with her hair piled up, then changed into a denim skirt and a soft cotton sweater and slipped into her favorite moccasins. After a day like today when she traipsed over half of creation, bare feet would have felt better. But she knew the fellows downstairs were making a production number out of dinner, so she was determined to join them in their efforts.

It was just getting dusky outside when she went out and lit the lanterns in the screen-sided tent. Then she slipped into the kitchen.

"You look nice," Matt said.

"Thank you. So do you."

He had cleaned the tomato sauce off himself, his son and the room. Both of the Viviano men were in clean blue jeans and Matt had apparently shaved again. There was a large flat pan resting on top of the stove. "It has to sit about fifteen minutes once you're done baking it before you cut it," he said, following her gaze.

"How long does it have to go?" The smells in the kitchen were making her even hungrier than she'd been when she came downstairs.

"About five minutes. Just enough time to pour us each a glass of Chianti and have Jory toss the salad." He got out the bottle and glasses and poured. The rich red of the wine looked like rubies and garnets in Larissa's glass and tasted like sweet sorcery.

Jory took his job seriously, mixing the glossy greens and tomatoes. "Where are we going to eat, Dad? You said Larissa had something up her sleeve."

Larissa chuckled a little. "I do. A hideaway in the forest." She motioned toward the back door. "See if you can find it."

Jory picked up the large wooden bowl and headed for the door. "As long as you don't let the bugs get in our lasagna. That thing is a bear to put together. Next time Grandma has us over for dinner, I'm going to kiss her."

He was properly appreciative of Larissa's hideaway. "This is neat. I forgot we had a screen house."

"It was in the garage all kind of wadded up on a shelf."

"One of the flood casualties last year," Matt said. "I kind of pitched things wherever, I guess, and I haven't ever gotten back in the far reaches of the garage to sort out."

The lantern she'd hung cast a soft glow on the inside of the tent, whose sides were all screened to let their dining area blend in with the trees at the back of the property where Larissa had pitched the shelter.

Inside she'd done her work as well. Even Matt's eyes glowed in appreciation by the lantern light. "We couldn't just have such a splendiferous meal on old picnic benches," she chided. "I thought since we were eating Italian tonight, we could eat like the very old Italians. The Romans." Larissa turned to Jory who looked as if he expected a lesson but had the good grace to appear interested.

"They ate on couches, kind of leaning on stuff. They had servants to feed them grapes and things, but we're going to have to do that part ourselves." It was enough that she'd set up the cots she'd found in the garage and decked them with pillows from around the house so that they flanked the low table.

"That's okay. I don't even like grapes that much anyway. I'll go get the bread," Jory said.

An hour later Larissa was stuffed silly and relaxed into bonelessness. "Well, Matt, you've ruined me for life. I don't think I'll ever be able to eat that frozen stuff and call it lasagna again."

His answering grin was wicked. "It's worth all the dishes, isn't it? But only if we're having more than the two of us. That's the only drawback. There just is not a small recipe for lasagna. We've got enough for another meal for the three of us, and another pan this size that will go in the freezer.''

She turned to look at Jory. He was reclining on his cot, watching the lightning bugs outside the screen. ''Want to catch a couple and let them go? You've got just enough time before I hustle you up to bed.''

''Okay.'' He was out of the tent in a flash. Matt stood up and extended a hand to her.

''It was hard enough getting out of this thing myself. It you're really that full you could probably use a hand.''

She didn't argue. His grasp was firm as he pulled her to a standing position. In the half dark of the tent it was nice to stand this close to him.

Larissa wondered if anyone else on earth had ever smelled this good, with the herbs from the kitchen blending with Matt's normal woodsiness. ''I noticed there was still a little more of that Chianti,'' she said. ''Should we knock it off once I put master Jordan to bed? Or better yet, how about you put him to bed for a change and I'll do kitchen duty. After a whole day off I sure don't mind.''

Matt looked grateful. ''I don't get a chance to tuck him in very often. Sounds like I'm getting the best end of this swap.''

''I don't know. He'll be pretty wound up after today. It was a very special day, Matt. Thank you.'' Larissa picked up a tray full of used dishes and headed for the house before she could get sappy and say anything else. The evening had been sort of magic, what with the low lights and good food and wine. No sense messing it up now.

It didn't take her long to set the kitchen to rights and put away the leftovers. She fixed a tiny plate of the cookies they'd bought that morning and went back out to the tent to pour two glasses of wine and wait.

She could hear the two of them rumbling around upstairs even from outside. It was such a mild night that Jory's window was open a crack and she could hear the whooping going on that constituted being put to bed. It didn't sound particularly restful or relaxing to her, but then she wasn't a little boy doing male stuff with his dad. She hoped there weren't any pillows to stitch up in the morning. Of all the tasks she'd gotten herself into as temporary housekeeper, sewing was the one she'd just as soon avoid.

Eventually the noise stopped in the house and the upstairs lights went off. A few moments later Matt was crossing the lawn.

"Got him settled in?"

Matt chuckled. It was a nice, warm sound in the darkness. "Yeah. He just about whomped me in a pillow fight, but I think he's finally asleep. Or close to it."

"I poured your wine. And made us a plate of these cookies. Although I can't really imagine being hungry enough to eat one," Larissa admitted.

"I guess I'm still a growing boy, because I've got room." Matt plunked himself down on a cot. "This was a neat idea. We haven't used most of the camping stuff in a while. Last summer, with the flooding and everything, was just too busy almost up until frost. And this spring we seemed to be playing musical housekeepers."

"Then I'm glad I got this much of it out. You must have quite some stack of gear."

"We do. Another tent, a regular one about this size, sleeping bags, the whole bit. You camp much yourself?"

"Never, really. I wasn't a Girl Scout or anything as a kid. And out in the country where I grew up it didn't seem like much of a treat to go sleep outside. Seems like we spent half the summer outdoors anyway, in the garden or the orchard or something. Plus anytime we had company, I'd sleep out on the screened-in porch in nice weather on what Aunt Stell called a pallet with the other kids. That was close enough to camping for me."

"No brothers or sisters?"

Larissa shook her head, then realized it was probably too dark for Matt to see her do that across the tent. "Only child. And my folks were killed in a car accident when I was about five, so there weren't any more. My great-aunt Stell took me in."

"I'm sorry."

"Don't be." Matt was the first person in years that she'd shared this much family history with. "It wasn't that bad. Stell hadn't ever had kids and we got on with each other just fine. And she knew more stories than anybody else I ever knew."

"Is that where you got them?"

"Some. I think what I got mostly was a love of any story as long as it was a good one. Which makes me think. How did you know about the horse, anyway?"

"Nonna told me that one. My grandmother. She lived with us when I was a kid. Unlike you, I lived with this huge group of people. My parents, two sisters, Nonna after I was four, and whatever relatives happened to be visiting at the time. There were always wall-to-wall Vivianos. Grandma's job was to keep the kids out from underfoot while Mom kept the place clean and everybody fed."

"Hence the story."

"Hence a lot of stories. She called yours *Gilette of Navarre*, though. I found it once in a book."

"I've found it in a couple books," Larissa told him. "Which one did you hunt up?"

"The *Decameron* by Boccaccio. You'd probably like it. I've got a copy of it somewhere in the attic."

Somehow during this conversation Larissa realized they'd begun to share a cot. Matt's weight combined with hers made them both slide toward the middle until their shoulders were touching.

He was still holding a glass with about an inch of wine in it and hers was empty. She definitely had to pin the light-headed, warm and drowsy feeling she was experiencing on the deep red wine. It couldn't be just the late summer night and the closeness to Matt. Could it? He was still telling her about his book.

"It's full of stories. Some are like Gilette and some are just plain silly. And a few couldn't be told to grade schoolers no matter how you worked on them."

"Oh? Now why do I bet those pages got a workout in your volume?"

His answering chuckle was throaty. "Hey, I was a college kid. And most of what I was studying was biology. It is kind of difficult to make something interesting out of the life cycle of the bullfrog. Better the fantasies of a bunch of old Italians telling stories while keeping themselves away from the Black Plague."

Larissa shivered. "That's kind of gruesome."

Matt shrugged. "Not really. Isn't that what we do with most stories? Keep ourselves from thinking about the grim stuff out there on the other side of the darkness? I mean, look at Jory. When it thundered, he wanted a story. And when he's sick in bed, he wants a story. Just like the rest of us. When things get too rough, we want a story."

His voice had gotten softer, and closer, with each argument. They were so close together on the cot now that you couldn't have put one page between them, much less a whole story. "So, Larissa," he said in a voice tinged with velvet. "Tell me a story."

Larissa opened her mouth, not knowing what she would have said. Before she could speak, his mouth was there on top of hers, telling a wordless story that was as old as the darkness that enveloped them.

The wineglasses were forgotten. There was just Matt, and herself and the night noises around them. His lips tasted of red wine as he explored hers, alternating nibbles with deeper forays into the most sensitive parts of her mouth.

His hair was every bit as soft as she'd imagined it and even thicker than she could have guessed when she tangled her fingers into it. Somehow during the kiss he'd pulled her up into his lap and his mobile fingers were tracing patterns on her spine.

It was probably only a few minutes of this that drove Larissa into breathless dizziness. She had never felt more reluctant to stop anything in her life than the kiss she pulled away from. "I can't tell you the rest of this story, Matt. I have no idea how it ends."

In the dark she could just see the shine of his eyes as he released her. He swallowed, hard. "Me neither, Larissa."

With that they let go of each other and Larissa fled to the sanctuary of her room.

Chapter Six

"It had to have been the Chianti," Larissa told herself in the mirror. Why else would she have let herself get that out of hand with Matt? She seldom if ever drank, and never strong red wine. Surely without that influence she wouldn't have thrown herself into his arms like that. Even the memory of the incident made her blush. She wished the blush came from being embarrassed over the whole thing. If it did things would be easier to resolve this morning.

Instead, looking at that face in the mirror, she had to admit that she wished she was seeing another reflection beside hers. From her mirror she could see her whole bedroom, including the rumpled narrow bed where she'd slept fitfully the night before. How nice it would be to see a distinctly masculine form in that reflection, still stretched out and taking up most of the bed. He was probably a slow waker. Those hazel eyes would be heavy lidded in the morning light, sunlight making gold glints in his brown hair and the fur she knew traced down his chest. She could just see the slow, easy smile that would be in her mirror, behind her shoulder, as she stood in her cotton gown and brushed her hair while he watched.

"Oh, stop it," she told herself. "This isn't going to happen, now or ever. It was the wine pure and simple." She put her hairbrush down hard on the dresser and went looking for nice serviceable boring clothes that would remind neither of them of the night before.

In the kitchen she stirred together the makings for waffles and heated up the waffle iron. Jory would come down hungry after a Saturday of activity. True to prediction, he bounced down the stairs about fifteen minutes after she did, already dressed in jeans and a sweatshirt.

"Oh, boy, waffles! Dad never makes those. He says they're a pain."

"They kind of are, homemade, but they're worth it. They're even better with cinnamon apples on top. Want to help?"

"Sure." His eyes sparkled with the prospect. Larissa got him set up peeling and slicing apples on a chopping board and putting the slices in a measuring cup until he had enough to feed the three of them.

While he was still at work Matt came down. Larissa nearly laughed when he appeared, barefoot and in a grungy old T-shirt with his jeans. Apparently she wasn't the only one who had decided to be unattractive for safety's sake. Or perhaps he was as slow a waker as she had imagined and he just didn't have the energy to haul himself out of bed and get all perky this early.

"Should he be doing that?"

"And good morning to you, too, Mr. Viviano," Larissa said. "Jory has had plenty of training in kitchen work the last month or so, and he's ready to graduate to using a paring knife. You'll notice that it is just sharp enough to do the job, and no sharper. And that he's listened well to all instructions, including those about cutting away from himself. Instead of fretting over him, would you like to contribute to breakfast by brewing a pot of coffee? You especially look as if you would appreciate it."

By the end of her windy speech, Larissa could see Matt melting from worry to ease in front of her. "Okay. Point taken. I'm kind of a bear early in the morning, especially when I've been on weird shifts. And yes, I'll be happy to make the coffee."

Of course he did it slowly and methodically, grinding beans and looking for a filter and filling the pot. Everywhere he parked himself seemed to be right where Larissa needed to be. The grinder sat directly over the cabinet where the cast iron skillet for the apples was. And the beans were stored next to the cinnamon, both of which they needed at once.

Larissa nearly ground her teeth in frustration. He smelled wonderful and looked as softly rumpled as he had in her early-morning fantasy. Why hadn't she ever noticed how delicious Matt was in the morning? Probably because she hadn't gone to bed thinking this intensely about him on other nights, and then found herself literally bumping into his soft jeans and hard muscles this early in the day.

Only once did Matt remark on their proximity. "What now?" he asked the third time they came together. He narrowed his eyes and looked Larissa up and down. Then he turned to the countertop in front of him, picked a large wooden spoon out of the container there and handed it to her. "Done now?"

"All finished. I'll go away and leave you alone."

"Don't go too far away. We've got stuff to talk about." His voice was low enough so that Larissa suspected that Jory, concentrating on the Sunday funnies at the kitchen table, didn't hear him.

"What kind of stuff?" She managed to stay calm and collected enough not to dump the apple slices outside the skillet.

"Last night. I'm really sorry, Larissa. I let things run away with me. I guess it was the wine. I don't drink much and—"

She was brandishing the wooden spoon at him in an instant. "Don't go giving me that routine, Matt. We can't blame all of what happened last night on one straw-wrapped bottle. Or even the stars and the lantern light or—" Before anything dripped off her spoon, Larissa collapsed in a fit of giggles.

Matt regarded her with the look of someone humoring the mentally ill. "What's happening with you, Larissa?"

In the midst of her giggle fit, Larissa was touched to hear the softness in his question and see the concern in those hazel eyes. "Oh, nuts. I tried to tell myself all this same stuff this morning. It was the wine, the night air, the novelty of dinner. Heck, Matt, it wasn't any of that. It was us."

"It was?"

"Yep. Can't blame it on the wine or the night, I don't think. Eventually we would have done this. Guess we can just call it the animal part of life."

Larissa went back to stirring her apple slices before they scorched.

"Animal, huh? So you're saying this would have happened eventually no matter what, because we're just acting on our animal nature?"

"Something like that. Now if you were a bear and I were a fox or something, it probably wouldn't have, because we just wouldn't be compatible. But we're both cougars or something and it just finally clicked."

Matt was shaking his head. "I swear, Larissa, the only thing weirder than this explanation is the fact that I understand it. And I'm half tempted to agree with it. But what are we going to do about it, woman?"

His soft voice was getting intense enough in tone that Jory looked up from his comic pages for a moment. The adults didn't look like they were doing anything more interesting than making breakfast so he went back to reading.

"Not a solitary thing, Matthew. Nothing else would serve a purpose between the two of us. Not here and now, at least. Now, how many waffles do you think you'll want?"

"Three." Matt looked mightily relieved. "Somehow I've seemed to work up a powerful appetite. For waffles." And he went in search of coffee cups while Larissa let the cinnamon steam from the apples bathe her flushing face.

It was just too quiet. At least that was what Matt told himself. He'd gone back to a week of crazy shifts, taking over more than once for somebody else before or after his own stint, so that he put in ten-hour days on the river about six days in a row. Larissa hadn't complained at all, merely murmured, "How convenient for you," the last time he'd broken the news to her, and gone on with her infernal knitting.

So maybe it *was* convenient. He needed to put some distance between him and Larissa until he sorted out the confused mass of feelings that threatened his normal calm. The funny part of all this was that even though Matt felt as if he'd been riding a roller coaster, his life was actually smoother than it had been in years.

There were clean shirts in his closet anytime he reached for them. Jory appeared well fed, clean and ready for a bedtime story or some play time whenever Matt got home at strange hours. His meals were always waiting for him, including things that hadn't been seen inside the Viviano household in recent memory, such as homemade bread.

That particular treat had nearly bowled him over the Saturday he'd dragged his sorry carcass in after another ten hour stretch. It had included a near fistfight with a couple of guys who were really tanked and still maneuvering the river, and a little stint of wading in after an illegal party of fishermen who disliked the appearance of someone official in their midst. He was wet and exhausted when the door opened onto the unmistakable odor of fresh bread just out of the oven.

Jory had been the one to remind him to wash up before sitting down to the glowing golden loaves in the kitchen. "Dad, you're so muddy-awful we should get the garden hose," he said between fits of giggles. "What did you do, go looking for tadpoles? Don't you remember they don't show up in the fall?"

"Jordan, it isn't nice to tease anybody that bone tired," Larissa had scolded in a good-natured tone. "Let Daddy get his hot shower and then we'll have the bread all ready for him, won't we? Should we share that honey we found in Augusta this afternoon?"

Jory had pulled back, eyes twinkling, in mock consideration. "Well, maybe. But only if he washes his hair, huh, Larissa?"

"Even if he doesn't," she'd told the boy. Hearing her indulgent tone of voice had nearly sent Matt over the edge. This was what family life was supposed to be about. A warm, smiling woman in a kitchen that smelled like bread. Damn shame that it would all evaporate one of these days and leave him poorer than he'd been before.

That was his expectation. That one day he'd come home and Larissa would be ready to leave. The routine would have gotten to her, or there would be one critter too many in a pocket, or just his ornery self would finally displease her once too often and she would go back to being just a librarian. That had to be much more pleasant, or at least more restful.

For now, though, it was too quiet. Things were restful when he expected them to be stirred up. Even now, as he climbed out of the truck onto the crunching gravel, the house looked awfully good. Too good, really. The porch looked as if it had been swept and there were mums growing there he didn't remember planting.

It was quiet when he unlocked the front door but that didn't surprise him. If it wasn't close to a mealtime, Larissa and Jory would be out wandering in the woods or up messing around with her computer or a myriad of other things. They weren't going to be hanging around waiting for him to come home because that was too chancy a proposal anyway.

It smelled like cooking in the hall. Something with basil and oregano, but then that could be just about anything from pasta to vegetable soup. Once Larissa had discovered the half-wild herb garden out back, she'd taken to raiding it frequently.

Still there was something different, nagging. The hall table was dusted and the mail, what little there was for him to pay attention to, was in a basket with a ribbon on the handle. That was new. Oh, well, one basket out of petty cash wasn't going to break him. He didn't think that was the cause of the feeling that was teasing his consciousness. Something more important than that was going on, and he couldn't figure out what it was.

He looked into the living room and stopped dead at the threshold. Here it was. The something that was nagging at him. A set of brand-new living room chairs. The damned room looked like a parlor. Polished wood, the real stuff shining with lemon oil. And it appeared that when Larissa blew the budget she went all out on the best upholstery, too. And matching pillows. This was it.

She could invade his home and cook like a chef. It was okay that there was fresh applesauce and homemade bread on the table. And that his son knew forty-seven ethnic folktales in their original form and now handled sharp instruments on a daily basis and made his own phone calls.

It was even okay that there seemed to be an order imposed on the general chaos around here. That everything ran on a schedule that wasn't his and was subject to change if the monarch butterflies migrated through the backyard. Matt still wondered how Larissa had worded that little note when Jory was without homework the next day. But redecorating without even consulting him was too much.

He put his things down on the floor next to the desk. Even that had been touched. All the flotsam and jetsam that usually poured into untidy piles was straightened and put in several trays on one side of the large wooden desk. And somebody had dusted and lemon oiled it as well. It almost made him want to growl as he went up the stairs.

Once up there he could hear them giggling over something at the computer. "I like that one, Jory," Larissa said. "Now, why don't you set it up to print out so we can show your dad when he gets home?"

"Already here," he said from the doorway. It was such a cute little domestic scene he hated to ruin it. Larissa was in an overstuffed chair in the corner. Come to think of it, that one didn't look familiar, either. She was knitting again, it seemed. If she was working on a sweater it ought to fit a basketball center by now. And Jory was up on his knees working at the computer.

"Oh, hi, Dad." Jory scooted off the chair and went to hug Matt. He dropped down to bring himself to his son's level, savoring the sprinkle of freckles for a moment and his vibrant grin. It was almost a shame to chew out the woman who kept that grin so permanent. Still, he had to keep control of his own house.

"Hi, sport. I hear you've got something for me there. Why don't you go put it down on my desk and I'll look at it after I check your homework, okay?"

"Homework? Like the stuff I haven't done yet?"

"That's the stuff. Why don't you rectify that little matter while I talk to Larissa, okay?"

"Okey-dokey." Jory didn't seem upset to leave. Matt could hear his door shut behind him.

"Since when does he need the door shut to do homework?"

"Since his teacher stressed the idea of a calm environment. I can't imagine things getting any calmer than this house stays most of the time, but there's no telling Jory that." Larissa smiled at him with an expression that would have made Mona Lisa jealous. "You wonder where he gets that little trait, don't you?"

"Not for a moment. And I guess that's a nice smooth lead-in to what we need to discuss." Matt found a chair he recognized and pulled it up close. "Nice chair you're sitting in."

"You like it?"

"Looks expensive. Like those two down in the living room."

"Is that your only concern? Expense? Because I have to break it to you, that growing boy across the hall is going to need a new winter coat pretty soon. The only one I can find doesn't reach his wrists."

"If that was a concern, why did you go out and buy a couple of chairs? I know I made a big deal about trusting you with finances around here, but dammit, Larissa..." Matt was amazed when her answer was to laugh. Hard.

"You really don't recognize any of them, do you?" Her mirth got the better of her again. "Dang, Matt, you're spacier than I thought you were."

"What do you mean?" It was hard not to growl.

"The chairs. All three of them are from that little army in the garage. I just cleaned them up—worked on the rough spots, and polished them up good. And that expensive upholstery? Remnants from garage sales and such. You really have been gone more than usual."

"So what did they cost you?" Matt started hauling out his wallet.

"I don't do one unless I can do it for under fifteen dollars." Why did she have to look so smug? "Don't bother with your old money. The look on your face just now was worth twice what I put into any of them."

"Yeah, I bet. I feel like an ass."

Larissa pointedly didn't say anything for a moment. "Of course, if someone would take me out to dinner tomorrow I could probably finish the love seat."

Matt nearly choked. "You got the love seat fixed too?"

"Aunt Stell never had any money," Larissa said. "And we never lacked for good things. You just have to know how to maneuver."

Matt knew in that moment that Larissa was an expert in the art of maneuvering. It was time to get out of her way before she mowed him down. He'd get the answer to his question and leave, quickly. "Where do you want to go to dinner, and what time?"

"Sunday dinner, three o'clock sharp. Jory's all yours until then, my friend. And we're going someplace I can get okra."

"Slimy stuff," Matt muttered as he turned away. He could still hear her giggling as he went down the hall.

* * *

True to her promise, Larissa did not appear until three the next afternoon. She used the time to straighten up her own quarters for a change, read some in a book she'd been putting aside, catch up on work she'd brought home and admit that she was falling hopelessly in love with Matt.

It wasn't that he was easy to love. He was the most obnoxious man when he wanted to be, which was often. But Larissa could see the roughness for what it was, a defense mechanism that was his outer shell against a hard world. At least he saw it as a hard world, and therefore he needed a shell.

Sometimes she felt as if she pierced it for a moment or two. Definitely out in the tent that Saturday night. He put up with things in her that she knew drove him nuts, like her storytelling and her fantasy. For someone as conservative and practical as Matt, she had to look like a loon. Still, he didn't protest much about all her strangeness.

In fact, Larissa suspected he welcomed it. What little he had said about his childhood led her to believe it had been warm and secure and filled with just the kind of nonsense she was trying to provide for Jory. And for that Matt seemed to be grateful.

Grateful wasn't enough to keep you warm at night, though. And grateful didn't last any longer than a scoundrel, which Larissa already knew. No, what she needed was someone much more than grateful. Putting on her dangly earrings, Larissa had to admit that what she felt was probably hopeless. If Aunt Stell were still alive she would counsel to leave things just as they were and be happy with the semblance of family life that Matt and Jory had provided. "Shame that I never did listen, isn't it, Stell?" Larissa murmured into the mirror.

Downstairs the men waiting for her looked sublime. Jory's hair was combed and slicked, making him look freshly washed. "I like the tie," Larissa told him. "It really makes you look dressed up."

"It's just my school pants," he said solemnly. "Dad tied the tie."

"Well, it certainly makes the outfit."

"How about mine?" Matt asked.

"Yours definitely makes the outfit," Larissa told him, straightening it a tiny bit. "And it's not even your school pants."

"Yeah, in my case the uniform just won't translate to Sunday wear. The department logo tends to get in the way." Nothing in Matt's present outfit got in the way. His dark blue denim shirt and patterned tie brought out the glinting highlights in his dark hair. Larissa in her twill skirt suddenly felt underdressed.

"Should I go change?"

"What for? You look fine."

"Yeah," Jory agreed. "Besides, I'm hungry. Dad didn't make a very fancy breakfast or anything and my stomach's growling."

Larissa looked at Matt in mock sternness. "Right. I make you responsible for one day and you starve the kid."

"What can I say?" Matt held out an arm like a proper escort. "You have me spoiled."

Larissa looked at him. Perhaps there was hope for him yet. He was beginning to tease easily instead of scowl most of the time. He probably still wouldn't eat okra. Maybe they could compromise on black-eyed peas.

As it turned out even Jory sampled the greens, black-eyed peas and okra Larissa got for dinner to satisfy a craving she couldn't have explained. He pronounced the greens "okay" and the okra "interesting." Larissa knew without asking that was the family code word for *weird*.

"So, I won't fix them at home. I notice you don't have any problems eating southern fried chicken," she pointed out.

"I like that better. And even the corn bread," Jory said. "Can I get ice cream?"

"Where could you possibly put it?" Matt looked at him in disbelief. "You must be developing a hollow leg."

Larissa shook her head. "This is just normal boy stuff. You should see what those cafeteria trays look like by fifth grade."

Matt got a lopsided grin. "Now that you mention it, I can remember the things my mother said about my appetite at that age." He looked at his son and Larissa could see that he was seeing him in a different light than usual. "He really is going to need that new coat, isn't he? And I bet a couple pairs of jeans. How about after the ice cream we stop off and get some of those things?"

Jory rolled his eyes. "Shopping." It sounded like a death sentence.

"Just for stuff you really need. It won't take long."

Larissa didn't even argue. She knew that shopping with two males couldn't possibly take long, even on a Sunday afternoon.

Jory was through with jeans and working on the winter coat selection with his father when she felt the tug on her sleeve.

"You're the story lady. From the library," the small voice said.

Larissa got down on the same level as the little girl beside her, which wasn't easy. The child was small even for the five that Larissa judged her. A narrow face framed with pale hair, faded but clean shirt, denim skirt. There was something about her that made Larissa's throat constrict.

"I sure am. Did you like that story?"

The child nodded. "I like *The Twelve Dancing Princesses* better. I heard it once on TV. Do you know that one?"

"I think so. My name's Larissa Camden. What's your name?"

"Kaylee."

So Larissa, watching both Jory and his father and a single woman with two boys slightly older than the girl work their way through the winter coats, told a story in which the twelfth princess, the sweet and kind one that eventually married the peasant boy who followed them all down in the caverns of delight, was of course Kaylee.

The child had a look of dreaminess on her face by the time her mother was ready to collect her. "I wondered where she had gotten to. I hope she didn't bother you too much."

"Not at all," Larissa told Kaylee's mother. If she thought the woman would have let her, she would have bought gloves to go with those two coats and the one she suspected the woman was going to have to provide for her daughter as well. But she knew it would look like charity to someone who wasn't disposed to taking it. So she had to settle for knowing her story had entertained a child who was often alone.

It took a hand on her shoulder for Matt to jostle her out of her reflections. "I said, are you ready to go? Who was that kid anyway? One of them from school?"

"No, from the library. The day I met you guys."

"The way you were looking after her, I would have guessed she was a long-lost relative instead."

"She kind of was. One I'd recognize anywhere." Larissa looked into his uncomprehending face. "There goes me about twenty years ago."

It wasn't until that evening, when Jory was settled down, the coffee was brewed and Matt was bringing her a cup to sit by the knitting, that he broached the subject again. He almost didn't broach it at all, because Larissa took control of the conversation when he sat down.

"You're sitting funny," she said.

"Yeah, hilarious. My side hurts." He lowered himself onto the couch all the way in a gingerly fashion.

"How long has it hurt?"

"I don't know. Off and on since I helped one of the guys shift an outboard motor last week."

"Ouch. Any swelling or anything?"

"None I can see. Looks just like the other side. Want to check?"

Larissa backed away from his suggestive grin. It was one thing to think about stroking his skin and quite another to be invited to play doctor. She was surprised how quickly thinking of one turned into the other in her mind. Flustered, she shook her head. "Not particularly. Just let me have my coffee, okay?"

"Fine." He let her sip in silence for all of thirty seconds. "That kid in the store. Did you tell her a story?"

"Yep. *Twelve Dancing Princesses.* It's not one of my regulars or anything, but she asked for it and I knew it."

"So you took fifteen minutes for a little performance for an audience of one."

Larissa took a sip of the coffee. It was too hot yet and she put it down. "Wasn't any problem. You were still busy and she wasn't doing anything. We did each other a favor. Nobody was bored."

"I can't imagine you ever being bored. You're like my grandmother—never truly still. Always talking or cooking or doing handwork or something."

"So maybe I wouldn't have been bored. But Kaylee sure would have been. And shopping with a bored kid is murder."

"Is that why you did it? For her mother?"

"No, I did it because she asked. I'm a sucker for anybody who wants to hear a story."

"You're probably a sucker for anybody who tells one," Matt said, not realizing how painfully his words hit home.

Larissa had to tell herself that he didn't mean them the way she took them.

"What did you mean about her being you? Were you that pointy and skinny?"

"Every bit. And every bit that much trouble in stores, I suspect. Of course we didn't go often, because Stell didn't have much money."

She finally put down her knitting so she could concentrate on talking to Matt. He looked so intent on listening that she felt she owed him as much. "My great-aunt raised me. My folks had married young, had me right away and always stayed, as Stell would say, poor as church mice. They lived with relatives, usually Stell, and never afforded better than an old rattletrap car. One day the old car ran into a truck. I was really too young to remember much besides my mama's pretty hair and my daddy whirling me around in the air.

"Stell tried hard. She was strict because that was all she knew. And looking back we probably never had two nickels to rub together. I still don't know how she kept me fed and clothed but she did it. Once I was old enough to figure out how tight things were, I went to work after school and on weekends."

"Not much of a childhood." It seemed to be a contrast to whatever Matt was remembering.

"Precious little. She was determined that I was going to be better equipped for life than my folks, or even than her. She was a bank teller in a town small enough it only had one bank. She framed my acceptance letter from the state university."

"Your graduation party must have been spectacular."

"She died of pneumonia my sophomore year, after Christmas break." It had been the coldest, longest winter Larissa had ever known. And she wasn't about to tell him that she'd gotten an extra copy of her diploma to put on that bare gray tombstone. No one else would ever understand.

She was surprised when the tears came and even more surprised when Matt was on the sofa with her, an arm around her shoulder. The whole day swam into perspective in an instant. "I miss her. It's silly—

it's been years and yet sometimes I expect to see her walk into the room with me."

The noise Matt made in his throat was almost a croon. "Oh, babe, do I understand. You cannot know how much." He patted her while her tears subsided. "Keep on telling the stories," he murmured into her hair. "If it gives you that childhood you missed the first time around, I'll let you tell as many as you like."

The kisses he feathered across her forehead were soft and comforting. They turned into something much deeper when he sought her mouth. Larissa was hoping he'd speak once he broke the kiss, but he stayed silent.

It was a while before Larissa calmed down enough to slip out of his arms. Until she did she felt cocooned in the firmness of his grip. But Matt true to being Matt, she was alone in the quiet once the tears were gone.

Chapter Seven

After what Larissa thought of as the Great Chair Uproar, things went fairly smoothly for several weeks. Too smoothly for her taste, actually. Matt was in and out often and didn't complain much about anything she did. It felt strange.

She was used to having him grouse about something. It didn't seem natural to put up fall leaf decorations in all the front windows of the house and have no one complain. Even when she and Jory cut out and iced several dozen cookies that looked like the autumn foliage outside and managed to stain the kitchen countertop bright orange in the process, Matt didn't complain. He did find the cleanser awfully quickly, but there were no complaints.

The only opposition came when Larissa suggested having Connie out to dinner. "Absolutely not. You don't need to entertain company with everything else you do," Matt argued. His pronouncement was so final she didn't even point out that Connie was hardly company.

"Besides, we're invited over there. At least Jory and I are, for a family thing in about ten days," Matt said.

"I thought you said Grandma invited all three of us," Jory said suspiciously. "What's a gauntlet, anyway?"

Larissa laughed while Matt looked at the floor. "It can be a heavy metal glove like knights wear. However I suspect in this case it's kind of like an obstacle course filled with people who want to grab you. And your dad is right, I'm not ready to run the relative gauntlet yet. I am only the hired help, not a prospect."

"What's a prospect? Is it like panning for gold? In social studies we're talking about guys who looked for gold in California."

Matt's lips were the ones twitching after that question. "Don't look at me," Larissa told him, pouring coffee. "You got us into this."

"A prospect? Yeah, it's something like panning for gold. Except sometimes you come up with gold and sometimes you come up with that gritty stuff from the bottom of the river that's like gravel only nastier."

Larissa considered pouring the rest of the coffee on his head. "Thanks heaps," she told him.

"You're the one who directed that one at me." Matt went on calmly drinking his coffee, never knowing how close he came to being a homicide victim. Or perhaps he was just loosening up, because Larissa found herself in these little sparring matches more and more frequently.

Even when Matt wasn't around she found herself having to defend him. Or her actions. Tess, when she saw her at the library story hour in October, was perfectly awful.

"It must be working fine," she said, surveying Larissa from all sides. "More than fine, I'd say. You've lost that haunted look."

"I never look haunted." Larissa stacked her picture books to put in her carryall.

"No, those purple raccoon circles around your eyes earlier in the summer were perfectly natural. And your favorite posture back then of looking over your shoulder just couldn't have been more comfortable, right?"

Larissa finally gave up and lifted her hands in surrender. "Okay, so I'm comfortable there. Let me remind you that you were the one who was nervous about the whole thing."

"Mainly because I was afraid of what you would get yourself into. A widower who's never home, with a rattletrap old house and a kid. I mean, you could work yourself into an early grave that way, Larissa. But if you're working that hard it must agree with you."

"I'm only doing what I want. I'm probably a real bust as a housekeeper. Anybody on a cobweb scavenger hunt could find them aplenty at Casa Viviano, I'm sure. We bake a lot of cookies and stuff, and I'm getting a lot of practice on my story repertoire."

"With Jory?" Tess sighed. "He is such a sweet kid."

"What happened to his mother?" Larissa hadn't meant to ask, but it popped out.

"I don't know. Something years ago. I get the feeling it was violent, whatever it was. But beyond that . . ."

"Violent?" Just repeating the word made Larissa feel much colder than she should.

"Well, sort of. But not involving Matt or anything." Tess looked as if she were revealing a guilty secret. "Honestly, I just don't know anything more. Not even her name."

"Deanna."

"Well, it's a start. You could check newspaper morgues or something. Whatever it was, it had to have happened when Jory was less than three. That's really how long I've known him and it was old enough history then that the local gossips didn't fill me in. Or maybe they didn't know." Tess rested her chin in her hand, elbows on the library counter. "Sounds a little Gothic, doesn't it? Weird guy in an old house surrounded by mystery."

"Oh, get a life," Larissa said, taking an ineffectual swipe at her. "He's not weird, there's no real mystery and I'm positive that whatever happened to her, she's not locked up in the attic. Remind me not to ask you any good questions again."

"Will do. Now let's figure out where to go for coffee after story hour, okay?"

"Sounds better." And with that, feeling no more relieved than she had before, Larissa went back to work.

"I want to be a prospect." Jory's statement the next week as he munched after-school cereal treats startled Larissa into wariness.

"You want to what?"

"Be a prospect. You know, like you and Dad were talking about. That hunted for gold."

"I don't think too many people do that nowadays, Jordan." Larissa tried to break the news that his career choice was a little outdated. At least he didn't want to be a knight.

"No, not for real. For *Halloween.*"

"Oh. That's a whole bunch easier." Her relief felt visible. Looking at his earnest little face, she had to admit the truth. What she had feared before had come true. She had fallen in love. Not just with Matt, but with his son and his house and his life. And she couldn't do anything that would hurt this smaller, more open version of the man she was growing to love.

Loving Jory was easy. He was all enthusiasm and scraped knees, like some perfect boy in her stories. And he loved those same stories so much. It broke her heart to think that someday she might be moving on and deserting him. That was why Larissa looked forward to each new escapade with him. When things wound to a close they would both have their memories.

"So, a prospect. Commonly called a prospector, sir." She tugged that dark gold hank of hair that was perpetually over his forehead. "How do we go about this? And remember, I am not the world's greatest seamstress."

"You did okay on the chairs so far."

"Yeah, but that's mostly just staples and glue and stuff. I can't staple your Halloween costume to your body. And if we glued it..."

"How would I get out?" Seeing that picture in his mind, Jory chortled into his milk. The spatter of bubbles that landed on the table made him go get a paper towel and mop up.

Yes, he was his father's son all right. He liked things orderly, most of the time. And he liked to run the show without being told what to do. That was probably why she liked both of them so much and was so aggravated at the same time, Larissa decided.

"Finish up your snack, then get some scratch paper," she told him. "While I get started on dinner, you're going to draw us a prospector."

Larissa peeled vegetables and Jory asked questions and drew. She chopped up everything she had peeled until there was the makings of a pretty good stew, and still Jory was drawing. She began to get a little nervous when the stew was simmering and Jory was still drawing, on his third sheet of paper. Finally she put the lid on the pot and sat down to see what she had gotten herself into.

He was still up on his knees in the kitchen chair, drawing. "This one is a close-up of all the gear and stuff. I know I need a pan, to pan for gold. And a mess kit. And maybe a really neat knife or a gun or something."

"The pan's easy. We can monkey around with a pie plate and come up with what we need," Larissa told him. "I'm pretty sure there's a mess kit in the garage in all that other camping stuff. But I don't know about the weapon part, sport. What's Dad going to say?"

His brow furrowed in such exact imitation of his father that Larissa could hardly keep from laughing. Had Matt been a serious, thoughtful child like this? Of course he had. How could he grow up into such a serious thoughtful adult otherwise? She thanked her lucky stars for getting involved with both of them. Never had she considered testing the merits of a man by looking at his son, but in this case they were so alike that it worked like a charm.

Jory was enough like his father he knew the answer to her question without thinking long. "He's not going to like that. Maybe if I bought myself a rubber knife out of my allowance, or made something out of cardboard. As long as it doesn't look too real."

The hair Larissa ruffled was so soft. It would hurt his manly pride to know that, so she kept the information to herself. "Good idea. And I've got another suggestion. Let's keep this to ourselves for a little while, okay? You know how your dad thinks we're being silly most of the time with all our plotting and planning. If he has to listen to this at the supper table every night he'll get awful tired of it awful quick."

Jory nodded. "You're right. We can show him when it's done."

"Which I hope is soon. Let's see the rest of this getup. I hope we can do most of it with things around here, Jory."

"Because you don't sew. And I don't like glue." His teasing smile brought out a dimple off center in his chin.

Even without constant discussion it was hard to keep a project of that size under wraps, but somehow the conspirators did just that. Matt shook his head more than once about the giggling and whispering that seemed to vanish when he appeared. "My birthday isn't until January. And there are no other holidays around. And you finished the love seat, so I don't have a clue," he said one night while drying the dinner dishes.

"You'll see. But not yet." Larissa watched him putting away the heavy cast-iron skillet she had cooked in. "You sure you're all right?"

"Just old age creeping up on me. It seems to be creeping faster than usual lately." He did seem stiff as he straightened up. "I may have to go to the doctor."

"Oh?" It was hard not to feel a little flutter of panic. For someone as self-reliant and macho as Matt to admit to the need of medical intervention, something must be wrong.

"Yeah. That ache from shifting that motor doesn't seem to be going away. Not all the way. It pulls or something when I'm getting out of a low chair, or lifting something."

"Like a cast-iron skillet."

"Or a box of regulation pamphlets, or anything else." He looked puzzled. "I still don't see anything. I mean, one side of my, uh, stomach looks just about the same as the other...."

"I'll take your word for it." Larissa had a sneaking suspicion she knew what was going on. However, what she would say wasn't what Matt would want to hear. "Do me a favor, though, and make that doctor's appointment. Set everyone's mind at ease, okay?"

Matt groaned. "You and my mother. She said the same thing. I should have taken you with us this weekend, you know."

"What for?"

"To give her and my sisters something to talk about instead of noticing I was acting laid up."

"Wonderful. Now I've moved from the hired help to a diversion."

"Your expression is priceless. Remind me never to really offend you, okay?" Matt's voice was soft and low, so close to Larissa's ear that her mouth got dry.

"You're tickling my ear."

"I can think of better ways." He leaned in to prove that he could. And then he started proving it. If Larissa's skin tingled before, the sensation he provided with his mobile mouth was indescribable.

More and more, being alone with Matt led to little encounters like this. It was why Larissa had become an expert at avoiding being alone with him. Each time he touched her she came closer to losing her reason altogether. And with all the challenges Matt provided she needed every ounce of her brain power to keep from making a terrible mistake.

"You certainly can. And I'd like nothing better than to stay here and let you prove it some more. But there's a dozen other things demanding our attention, like Jory's homework and his bath, and my quarterly supply lists."

Matt's breath in her ear went from tickle to sigh. "Spoken like a diversionary expert. My sisters would have had a field day."

"I'm sure they would have," Larissa said to the empty air once he left. It was one of the main reasons she'd been glad to have been left out of the gathering.

The other had been more nebulous and much scarier. As she wiped down the kitchen counters and tidied up for the evening Larissa kicked herself for not finding a way to be included. Maybe then she could have found out about Deanna. Who she had been, what had happened to her. If she was as beautiful and competent as Larissa imagined her.

She had to have been something extremely special for Matt to still be hanging on to her memory the way he was after—what had Tess said—almost five years? In her mind's eye Larissa was building such a paragon that she knew she'd never measure up, no matter how long she lived in Deanna's shadow.

Deanna would never have made errors in judgement like she had in the past year. She probably lived a well-ordered life with her handsome husband and perfect toddler and did it all right. All except whatever she'd done last. Whatever it had been, it had taken her suddenly. And her husband still, more than a little, blamed himself for it happening. Larissa found herself shivering a little when she turned out the kitchen light.

Friday was a perfect fall day. A golden day. It was the only way Larissa could describe it. Shades of gold painted the trees outside and burnished the library windows with sunbeams. Everything felt heavy and lazy with fall. Perhaps that was why she let the kids talk more than usual while they checked out their books. "And they have these great hats and stuff. Including one with a tail!" she heard one fourth grader tell another.

She was there in a minute. The boy looked as if he were expecting a reprimand. His mouth actually dropped open in surprise when she asked him for directions to his favorite store instead.

Jory couldn't imagine where they were going after school. Larissa let him guess all the way to the antique shops and craft places that made up Old Town St. Charles. He seemed mystified when they got there.

"This is a boring place, Larissa. They have lady stuff and junk. Why are we going here?"

"You'll see." She counted addresses and was a little confused herself until she saw the shop she wanted facing an alley instead of the main street.

Inside Jory stood silently. "Wow. Prospector heaven."

"Yeah. But let's not blow our budget. I figure the chores you've helped with the last month have earned about . . . seventeen dollars," she said, pulling a figure out that would probably match the meager cash reserves in her purse. Her charge card was still recovering from the battering it had taken in the spring. Even Jory would not convince her to get into financial trouble again.

He fingered the pelts on the wall of the store and gaped at the photographs of the mountain men dressed in their skins. The smell of leather pervaded the shop along with the smokiness of pipe tobacco. It felt as if they'd stepped back at least a hundred years, especially when Larissa noticed the gentleman manning the tall counter in his fringed buckskin shirt.

By the time they were back outside on the cobblestone walk clutching their bag of purchases she and Jory were both in high spirits. "Let's go home and put it all together. This is going to be so cool," Jory said.

"Okay, hold your horses. We've got just enough money left to each get a cookie at that place across the street. Care to join me?"

"Sure. Can I have chocolate chip with nuts?"

"As long as you eat dinner. Your dad will have a cow if he sees you poking around at your food and I tell him we pigged out on cookies at five o'clock."

"Okay. Hey, Larissa, I've got you doing it."

"Doing what?" His hand felt companionable as they crossed the street.

"You said Dad would have a cow."

"Well, he's too big to have kittens."

Jory laughed all the way through his cookie.

He was still in high spirits when they got home. Larissa was glad there was already a casserole of frozen chicken pie waiting to be put into the oven for dinner. Even through the five minutes that she spent putting that together Jory hopped around the kitchen, shifting impatiently from foot to foot. "Come on, Larissa. I want to put on my costume."

"We're going to do it, Jordan. How about going up and putting on those jeans we picked out and a T-shirt for your foundation. Then we'll work from there."

He was up the stairs in a flash and down before Larissa had everything out of the bag. "Ready."

"Then go to that bottom cabinet over there and get the dented pie plate. The one we've been saving just for this."

"I just hope Dad didn't throw it out," Jory said, worry creasing his small forehead. "You know how he gets rid of stuff."

"I do. Let's hope he's been too busy." Matt did have a habit of discarding things the moment they were no longer of use, or perhaps even before Larissa would have thrown them away herself. It went a long way toward explaining why Deanna was such a mystery. Larissa had a sneaking feeling that by the time Matt would have wanted to save mementos, there was nothing left to save.

She still kicked herself for not rescuing that Chianti bottle. It would have been just right on her windowsill with a dark green candle in it. Instead Matt had already put it in the bin to recycle with the rest of the glass, stripped of its straw case and label by the time she'd thought of it the next morning. Even now, weeks later she could remember the effects of the wine without the bottle. His silky hair under her hands, warm mouth hungry...

"Larissa! Let's go." She stopped her woolgathering to turn an impatient first grader into a forty-niner with nothing but a few strips of leather, some rabbit skin, scissors and some ingenuity.

"Step back and let me look at you." The smell of the baking pie filled the kitchen almost as broadly as Jory's smile. Larissa had to admit he looked wonderful. A miniature prospector. All he needed was a grizzled beard to look like the pictures in the books they'd found together. Larissa suspected they were pushing Matt's fantasy limits as it was. No sense in adding false hair.

She wondered what Jory had been other years for Halloween. Knowing Matt, it had been something like a ghost out of a pillowcase or something unimaginative. She pulled on the tail of their one extravagance, a coonskin cap. "So, is this better than last year's costume?"

"Yeah. I didn't have one. I wasn't old enough last year. But this time..."

Warning bells went off in Larissa's head, but she had no time to stop and consider. Instead, the kitchen door was open and Matt was standing on the rug. He didn't seem to be in a very good mood.

"Aw, rats, Dad. You caught us. You weren't supposed to see this yet," Jory groused. He still couldn't hide his pride and delight. "What do you think?"

"Very... period. You have some social studies project coming up? I know you have to do a report, but I didn't think Mrs. Clemens would make you go to such lengths."

"She didn't. I'm a prospect-or." Jory seemed doubly proud at remembering the whole word. "Larissa even let me get the knife for my belt with my allowance. She says it has to stay in the sheaf."

"Sheath," Larissa corrected mechanically. Most of her attention was focused on Matt. He hadn't moved from the doorway and seemed to look more confused and unhappy by the moment.

"We're going to get me a treat bag and dye it with tea so it matches my outfit. Did you know Larissa used to use a pillowcase?"

The child's chatter seemed to be more than Matt could comprehend. "Most of us use a pillowcase, Jory. It keeps our pillows clean."

The boy rolled his eyes. "Not for sleeping, silly. For trick-or-treating. To carry her candy."

"That's what this is all about? Halloween?"

Larissa didn't think she was going to like what was happening. Dread for Jory's fragile happiness kept her quiet and still.

"Well, you've gone to a lot of trouble for nothing, Jordan. You can wear that to school if you want, but that's it."

Jory had gone from frantic display of all his new treasures to unmoving disbelief. "But last year you said I was too small. I'm lots bigger. I'm going trick-or-treating, aren't I, Dad?"

Matt's eyes were flat and his voice even flatter. "Nope. Not now. Not next year. This time listen real good Jory. You cannot go trick-or-treating."

"I'll be the only one in my class who doesn't go." His lip was trembling suspiciously.

"I don't care if you're the only one on the continent that doesn't go. It's not going to change my answer."

Larissa's shock only grew when Matt, without any more discussion, walked out of the room.

"Dad, can't we . . ." Jory trailed after him.

He whirled on the little boy. "Jordan Michael. No. And no more arguing." He finally seemed to see Larissa. "And I hold you responsible for this fiasco."

He was gone again before Larissa could say anything back. Knowing that it was silly now to keep the oven at full power, she went to turn it off. Her fingers felt like wood.

"Jory, your daddy is right. I should have asked him," she began.

The boy didn't let her get any further. "No. He's not right. He's not right at all." The knife and belt clattered to the floor along with the coonskin cap before he rushed out of the room. Even though he made no noise Larissa could feel his tears as he went up the stairs. The bedroom door that slammed was an exclamation point.

Larissa walked up the hallway to the living room, knowing where she would find Matt. He was there, already going over papers at his desk.

"I've known you are reserved," she told him as he looked up. "And we've never seen eye to eye on raising that boy. But he's your son and I've never said anything. Until now.''

When Matt started to open his mouth she raised her hand. ''Let me finish. That was one of the cruelest things I've ever seen anybody do to a kid. He didn't deserve that.''

''Yeah, well, I didn't deserve to walk in here and find him thinking he was doing something I'd never even consider.''

''How was I supposed to know that? He's right, you know. There isn't another kid in his class that won't be going someplace Halloween night. At least to the mall or something.''

''Well, tough. He's not going. No use leading him on by letting him think otherwise.''

''He's a child, Matt. Did you have to be that blunt?'' Larissa was surprised at how loud they were both becoming. It was unnecessary, considering how close Matt had gotten when he stood to confront her.

''Yes, I did. It's one thing for you to encourage all his storytelling and his fantasy. It's another for you to flat out contradict the whole way I'm raising him. Life isn't fair. It isn't anything like the castles in the air you two build together. He needs to be brought back down to reality.''

Larissa pushed her hair out of her flushed face. ''But why? There's no good reason to tell him he can't go out with everybody else.''

''No good reason for you, maybe. I can think of several, none of which are your business.''

''That's just it. Nothing around here is my business, according to you. Nothing that counts, anyway.''

"So maybe this is all a mistake. We don't seem to agree on how to raise my son." His eyes were like flint. "Perhaps it's time for you to go back to being a librarian, Larissa."

She felt deflated. "Perhaps it is. Consider this two weeks' notice. Now."

Her legs were rubbery as she went up the stairs. It had been that sudden and swift. For a moment in the kitchen there had been two children there and she was one of them. Watching Matt shoot down Jory's dream, she knew she couldn't stay. Her own dreams were as fragile as the child's and Matt would shoot them down just as efficiently.

When she wiped tears off her face in her silent room it was difficult to decide who they were for. Most of them were for Jory, whom she was dying to go in and comfort. He was enough like his father that he would have pushed her away and it would just have made her cry harder. A few were for herself and for the foolishness she felt all over again for her part in all this. Why hadn't she even have guessed beforehand that Matt would react like this?

But most of her tears were for Matt. Because behind the anger in their argument she had found the anguish Matt wanted so badly to hide. Anguish that made him grasp at his son so tightly that Larissa knew that without something in between them they would fly apart. And no matter how badly she hurt, she wasn't ready to be that something.

Chapter Eight

When the knock on her door came later, it wasn't who Larissa had expected. She flung it open, ready to do battle with Matt. Instead, a tear-stained Jory walked in. She closed the door and they went wordlessly to the rocker. It was difficult to gather him up to sit in her lap. He was all bony elbows and long legs. Somehow they found a way to fit and only after they had found a comfortable rhythm did he say anything.

First he backhanded the remaining evidence of his crying off his face. "You can't leave. Not yet."

"I have to. Sometimes grown-ups—"

"Don't tell me that. You guys aren't even married. So you can't get divorced."

"It works the same way with people who just work together, Jory," she said softly. "Sometimes we can't get along." *And sometimes we get along too well,* she told herself silently. *For just long enough to screw up everybody's lives.*

"But you can't." His voice was urgent. "Dad's okay, but you understand stuff he doesn't. When I get lost, how will he find me if you're not here?"

"He's a good finder, Jory. I don't think you have anything to worry about."

The boy just shook his head and burrowed tighter into her embrace. "He won't know where to look."

She didn't have any comforting answer for that, so Larissa just rocked some more. "I wish I could tell you I was never going to leave. It would feel better for you. But I can't do that. This just isn't working out for me, Jory. It isn't you, or anything you've done."

"No, it's my dad." He said it just the way Matt would have, matter-of-factly, while Larissa knew it was scalding his insides the same way things did his father. So she kept rocking.

They were still there, with the room growing darker, when the knock she'd expected came. "Might as well come in," she called from the rocker.

Matt stood in the doorway.

"No, Matt. All the way in," she told him. "Tonight I'm not going to put up with your prowling around."

He came all the way into the room with that, and got to Jory's eye level in front of the rocker. "I owe you an apology."

Jory rubbed his eyes again, this time with the sleep that the rocking was inducing. "You mean you'll let me go trick-or-treating?"

"No. But I shouldn't have been so mean in the way I told you about it. Let me explain while I tuck you in."

"Will you carry me?"

"Can't. That's part of the explaining."

Jory's expression made it clear he understood as little as Larissa did, but he got down off her lap and went with Matt. She got up and stretched the stiffness out, then went back to the chair with her knitting. She knew that once Jory was settled, Matt would be back. It had been there, unspoken in his eyes.

She'd finished the last of the project she had been working on by the time he returned. They were going to look silly now, the matching vests she had made for the two of them. Not silly, exactly, but not as right as it would have been with the three of them going places together. She smoothed the last panel while Matt settled in the room's other chair. "So, talk."

"I went to the doctor today."

"Finally. Why do I get the feeling the news wasn't good?"

His smile was a little grim. "You had an idea, didn't you?"

"Yeah. Just because both sides looked the same didn't mean they were both healthy. Hernia?"

"Double. Due to be repaired next week. I've got enough time off lined up that I can take the two full weeks the doctor wants me to. But, Larissa, I won't be able to even walk around much the first couple of days. Or lift anything for the full two weeks. Or drive for five days...."

"I get the general idea. We'll make it three weeks' notice, all right?"

"I would appreciate it."

Larissa concentrated on the panels in her lap, ready to sew into vests. "So, explain to me why this all meant you came home and exploded."

He ran a hand through already rumpled dark hair. It was the most traumatized she'd ever seen Matt. And if she wasn't still so angry with him she would have wanted to go hug him.

"It's hard."

"I seem to remember somebody telling me life was hard."

The irony wasn't lost on Matt. "Right. I'll try. I've never been away from Jory overnight since Deanna died. And I've never been in a position where I'll be this vulnerable. I know it's only minor surgery, but it's scary. They have to put me out. What if something goes wrong? I'm all he has left."

That did it. She was over on the floor next to the chair in a blink. "I know. And you came home feeling all that and wondering how to tell us and here was Jory in his costume."

"Right. But I still shouldn't have come on so strong. It's just that I was already so tightly wound, and coming home to that. I hate to disappoint him..."

She patted his arm. "I almost understand. That's what's so annoying with you, Matt. Most of the time I almost understand. But never all the way."

"Guess it's best that you do leave then. Because I could say the same thing about you and it scares me silly."

It was fully dark before he got up out of the chair and left Larissa to go back to her sewing.

A week later, Larissa was still reviewing in her mind just how she got stuck doing this. The only thing more threatening than Matt healthy and walking around on his own was the thought of Matt needing her for everything. And the scariest part of the whole mess was that she wanted to do it. In fact, if she had been at her job long enough to build up time off, it would have been her taking him to the hospital for surgery that morning instead of Connie.

But she had only been on the job a matter of weeks and it didn't feel right to ask for time off that way. Besides, this way, she told herself, she and Jory could reassure each other through the day.

Matt was the one who looked as if he needed reassuring before daylight when they were both in the kitchen. "I'm thirsty," he groused."

"Just a few hours and you can have a drink."

"Just a few hours and wanting a drink will be the least of my problems." He looked like a man off to face the firing squad. He was wearing his oldest jeans, and he hadn't shaved. Larissa wondered again at the difference in men and women. If she had been the one on the operating table she knew she would have been fussing with her appearance for an hour before she left. "I think I need a hug," Matt said wanly.

"Might as well." Larissa crossed the space between them. "I know you won't pester me for one afterward. There won't be anyplace I can hug." She walked into his arms. It was a bittersweet thing now, because Matt's embrace still made her feel more whole than anyone else's ever had. Even now, when they were both planning their leave-taking he still felt like half of something that made a whole entity when joined with her body.

He hung on for quite a while. Larissa traced his bunched back muscles through his flannel shirt. "It's going to be okay. You'll see."

"Sounds like what you tell the first graders when they forget their books."

Her nose was still buried in the flannel that smelled uniquely of his cologne. "It is. But it never felt this good."

His hand was in her hair now. "Aw, Larissa. I'm scared. I don't want to do this."

"You'll be fine. Jory will be fine. We will all be fine. If you want, I'll call the hospital every time I get a free period to check on you."

"They won't let me on the phone even if I'm lucid."

"Yeah, I know. And I bet you won't be, either. Lucid."

"This is most likely true. But Mom will be lucid enough for both of us." He started to pull away from her embrace.

She gave him a squeeze before letting go. "I'll see you this afternoon."

"Early, hopefully." He looked around the kitchen. "Aren't you having breakfast?"

She shook her head. "Not yet. Once you and Connie leave..."

He smiled. "That's sweet, Larissa. You can drink coffee in front of me if you want."

"I won't."

"No, I should have known." His answering caress of her hair was incredibly gentle. "I should never have let you give notice."

"We can talk about that some other time. When you're not worried about anything."

This time his smile only lifted one corner of his mouth. "Right. That happens so often in my life." Before they could talk any more, the doorbell rang.

"Mom. I'll have her come in while I go upstairs and wake Jory up and get him going."

Connie came into the kitchen while Matt was upstairs. She looked concerned. "He's more anxious than I thought. It's just a little nip and tuck, isn't it? Is there something he hasn't told me?"

Larissa shrugged. "Only if he's not sharing it with me, either. I think it's the loss of control for a little while that's getting to him."

"That could be. Of all my kids, Matt is the one who always wanted to run the show. Any show, and all the time." She looked up. "And heaven knows he's had enough times where life has frustrated him in that effort. Don't worry, I'll bring him back in one piece. Repaired."

"Do that. I don't handle blood well. Let's make sure he's past shedding any when you turn him over to me, all right?"

"Will do." With a wave, Connie was off at her usual speed, leaving Larissa to listen to Matt's coming down the stairs, the opening and closing of the door and the starting of Connie's little car.

She shouldn't be so nervous herself, Larissa argued internally, smoothing a rumpled corner of her place mat. It was just a minor surgery. As she told Matt, they'd all be fine. But even as she told herself that again, she got such a nagging feeling of dread.

It wasn't that she was worried for Matt, not physically. He'd be home in the evening, probably acting like a bear with a sore paw. It was the fragile truce they'd all worked out together that seemed in the most danger to Larissa and she couldn't even tell why she felt that way.

Jory was in front of her in the kitchen before she heard him, making her gasp. "Whoa. Startled me there, sport. You're so quiet sometimes."

He grinned. "I practice. Can we eat breakfast at school? Friday is donut day."

"Sure." She pulled the brim of his ball cap over his face. "Why not live dangerously? Get your bookbag and I'll gather my stuff." It would alter the routine and give them something to think about besides Matt and his surgery. Besides, Larissa had to admit, she liked donuts as much as the kids.

"Dad, you're walking like a giant question mark," Jory told his father later that afternoon. Larissa had to stifle another laugh.

"We're both perverse," she told Matt as he shuffled back to the bed after his trip across the room. "If the doctor had told you not to cry we'd probably be finding everything tragic."

"Everything *is* tragic," he said through gritted teeth. "It's just striking us funny, is all. Naturally, since I can't laugh."

He could laugh. It was just that the effort contracted the very muscles that had been stitched and repaired. And of course, everything since Connie had settled him in and turned him over to Larissa had been hilarious.

Matt looked more vulnerable than Larissa had expected was possible. How anyone who was usually so gruff could relax so much was inexplicable. "Must be the drugs," she muttered, off to get a pitcher of ice water. It was the one thing he wanted.

Connie's lasagna, already in the oven, was probably going to get little attention. The lovely green salad she'd tossed while waiting for them to come home from the hospital would sit in the refrigerator. But ice water was in great demand.

So Larissa went to the kitchen and made another plastic pitcher up and brought it in. "Do you want me to sit here with you?" Matt was still standing next to the bed looking befuddled. "Or do you want some help?"

"Help. Once I figure out what I want help with."

"I think you were going back to bed." It was very difficult not to giggle again. Matt looked like an owl, and not a very happy one, with little tufts of his unruly dark hair completing the picture by sticking up at the temples.

"I remember that much. And I know what I want to do, only not how to do it."

Looking at everything, Larissa saw his problem. How was he supposed to climb back into bed comfortably without putting any stress on his incisions? Sitting down on the edge would be all right, but then he'd be stuck in that position. "What about just kind of crawling into bed?"

Matt scowled. "I guess I'm reduced to that." He'd changed into sweats and a T-shirt that were even more disreputable than what he'd worn to the hospital. They were very old and very soft. Larissa could see his bunched muscles under them where pain and discomfort were making him tense.

He shifted around, slowly, and climbed into the rumpled queen-size bed. And stopped on hands and knees, with a muffled expletive. "I'm stuck."

Larissa climbed into the bed next to him. It was still hard not to laugh. "Okay, lean on me and we'll both lower ourselves in here sideways."

The moment he complied she realized what a mistake it was. Not that she couldn't handle the weight of his broad back against her. No, she was overpowered in quite another way.

Even just home from surgery in awful old clothes, Matt felt wonderful. And here she was, easing them both down on his bed, his body cradled against hers. Only remembering that he needed help, not seduction, kept her sane.

"Oh, this is great," Matt said a few moments later. "Perfectly comfortable other than the fact I'm probably mashing you flat."

She was on the bottom of the pileup. Larissa thought that it was kind of like trying to hold Jory in the rocker. Matt in this position was all bones and bunched muscles that poked. And though he might have eaten very little for a few days worrying about the surgery, his weight on top of her was still impressive.

She eased out from under him where he lay on his side and watched him settle into a comfortable position. Larissa knew she should move. There was just too much danger in being stretched out on Matt's bed, even with him only hours past abdominal surgery.

Once he was relaxed he looked like one of those cats she was always teasing him about, lean yet massive, dangerous even in repose. If he'd had a tail, he would have been twitching it in aggravation. "You hurt, don't you? Why don't I get you one of those pills...."

"They make me sleepy. And dizzy. And even more thirsty than I am already." He was growling into the pillow. Larissa stroked the taut shoulders facing away from her until the tension in them eased a little.

"I'm sorry you're feeling so bad."

"Yeah, well, so am I. And I don't think it's going to get any better anytime soon. I hurt, and I itch. Those staple things they used to close everything up with made me swell."

"Staples?" Larissa felt a little queasy.

"Yeah. Wanna see? You may get to even if you don't want to, because tomorrow night I get to take a shower and take off the bandage and unless I feel a whole bunch different than I do now, I'm going to need help."

"Fun."

"No, but as long as I feel this bad I might as well spread it around." His voice was getting fainter.

"You going to doze off on me again?"

"We can only hope so. I think I'm better company that way."

Larissa was just glad Matt's back was to her and he couldn't see her nod. With a few more moments of rubbing, his shoulders relaxed completely and he was asleep. She slipped off the bed as gently as possible and tiptoed out of the room.

She had been wrong about her assessment before he came home. Taking care of Matt, sick, wasn't like taking care of a bear with a thorn in its paw. Bears eventually went off in a corner to lick their own wounds and shut up. This was going to be infinitely more challenging.

At least he woke up with something close to an appetite. Connie's lasagna was ready by then and she brought plates of it and salad into the bedroom for a picnic. Jory was enchanted.

"I've never eaten in a bedroom before," he said with a chortle. "This is cool."

"Never?" Larissa looked at Matt. "What about when you're sick? Doesn't your dad bring you breakfast in bed or something?"

"Never sick," Matt chimed in. "This is the first time I can remember either of us taking to our bed since....in years."

She could finish the sentence he hadn't, and could see that picture in her mind of a man suddenly bereft tucking a tiny little boy into bed with him to fill the gaping hole in both their lives. Jory didn't catch the reference and went right on eating on the blanket she'd spread out on the floor. Even Matt went back to his dinner. Not eating for nearly twenty-four hours had sharpened his appetite once it returned.

"Grandma's is better than yours. Sorry, Dad, if I hurt your feelings."

"No offense taken. Grandma's is better than mine," Matt told him.

"I'm not sure," Larissa told him. "There was something about eating yours, out in the tent, that had a certain charm to it we just couldn't duplicate." It was fun watching his slow answering smile as he remembered the evening.

When they were done Larissa and Jory cleared. "So, what do we do now?" Jory asked, bouncing back into the room. "I know it can't be anything much because Dad's supposed to stay in bed."

Matt, looking more calm than he had in days, stretched out against the headboard of his bed. "So, give us a floor show."

"What's that?" Jory stopped bouncing.

"Entertainment. Tell us stories. Dance. Something."

Jory sat down, cross-legged, on the floor. "Let me think." The process took a while. As he thought, Larissa made her way to the spot that Matt patted on the other side of the bed. She sat there in much the same posture as Jory. While they sat quietly, Matt's hand roamed her knee, idly stroking and caressing.

She watched it there, long strong fingers wandering. It was a good hand. One she wished she could hold on to for a long time. Maybe forever. Instead, she would have a few more weeks and then... It didn't bear thinking about. As if to distract her, Jory sprang up. "Okay. I've got my story. Now I just have to get in character."

As he left the room, Matt gave her a questioning look. "One of Ms. Clemens's ideas," Larissa explained. "They can dress up as the person they're giving a book report about, or anything like that. She says it gives them a new dimension in learning."

"Great. Now you're all conspiring against me." He didn't sound as glum as his words would have warranted.

"Not conspiring. Just trying to bring some sunshine into your incredibly dull life, Viviano." She rumpled his hair the way she would have Jory's. The feel of his hair under her fingers was delicious.

"Um. If what you're doing now is part of the sunshine, keep on." He almost purred under her hand. "I've got to admit that since you've been here there haven't been many dull moments, Larissa."

She made a wry face. "I'm told I have that effect on people."

Before he could reply Jory came back into the room, dragging a laundry basket full of props.

He stood in the middle of the floor in a dramatic posture.

"My story," he began loudly. "It's the story of the World's Greatest Hunter who Lived in Defiance." Larissa could hear the capital letters as he proclaimed the title. "He didn't use guns and he didn't use knives. He was a peaceful hunter."

The hunter was verbose if anything. As the story went on, Matt's clutch on her knee got tighter. Even when it reached the point where his grip threatened to cut off all circulation, she couldn't look at him.

The story droned on, with Jory going through a variety of motions and long, windy explanations. Finally Matt's strangled voice broke in quietly. "Uh, Larissa? Is this leading to where I think it is?"

The hunter had already dealt with a bear and a mountain lion and was moving on to wolf. Larissa shrugged. "I've never heard it before." The wall above Jory was beginning to be fascinating. It was the only place she could focus her attention that wasn't going to result in gales of laughter.

"Correct me if I'm wrong..." Matt's voice was still strangled, as if he were fighting as hard as she was not to explode. "But if the great hunter is going after things with a truck, doesn't that make the things he's bringing home and skinning and wearing and stuff..."

"Yep. The World's Greatest Road Kill." Even as she spoke, Larissa handed him the pillow behind her, pressing it firmly into his chest. She positioned it high enough so that it wasn't hurting his incision. He could do that himself when he cracked up, which appeared to be imminent.

"Jory, honey, why don't we take a break in the story and get Dad some ice cream." She ushered her dramatic charge out of the room just as the sounds, somewhere between a wheeze and a groan, began emanating from the bed. It was going to be a long weekend.

Larissa felt as if her eyelids had been sanded. Nothing else could possibly make them this scratchy. Perhaps the exercise in sleep deprivation that she'd been experiencing for thirty-six hours had helped.

Friday night had been uncomfortable but not unbearable. She'd insisted on sleeping on Matt's floor after he expressed fears he'd popped a stitch laughing. There was nothing seeping through the bandage, and he wouldn't take more pain medication until she nearly wrestled him into the pillows. Then he'd slipped off quickly into sleep. And proceeded to make the strangest set of small and large noises imaginable for ten hours.

He, of course, had woken up looking almost refreshed. Larissa had felt as if she had spent the night on gravel instead of just a lumpy sleeping bag on the floor. Jory looked brighter eyed and bushier tailed than either of them.

Once she was up, Larissa's day fell into a routine of feeding people, bringing drinks to the bedroom, finding amusements that kept Jory out of his dad's hair but not so far away he couldn't be watched, and talking to Matt.

He didn't want small talk and he didn't want anything challenging. Just a steady stream of conversation to keep his mind off itching. And hurting. And the crushing inactivity.

"You never sit still at work, do you?" Larissa finally snapped. "I'll bet you're like a cat on hot ashes all day."

He looked at her, his expression solemn. "You're right. I guess it's my way of keeping busy. I'm driving you crazy, I'll bet."

"Insane." She held up the vest she'd just finished stitching together. "Can you continue to drive me crazy, only sitting up?"

"Sure. I guess so." The position involved a little bit of struggle, but he finally got to the point of sitting on the edge of the bed.

"Great. Now let's slip this on over your lovely T-shirt. What do you think?"

Matt looked down. "It will go better with a blue button-down. Who's it for?"

"You, silly. There's one Jory's size still in the basket. If you stop bothering me I could probably get both of them done sometime today."

"Not that we're going anyplace soon where we can wear them. Unless they're waterproof."

"Waterproof? Not exactly."

"Well, rats. Because the only place I'm going in the near future is the shower. And you're definitely going to get to help."

Larissa's mouth felt dry all of a sudden. "Oh, joy. Maybe we should bring the World's Greatest Hunter back for an encore."

Matt glared. "Don't even think about it. I think last time I pulled a staple. Just get me into that warm water in one piece."

She nodded. He would be in one piece. Now if she could just say the same for her self-control. Larissa suspected that helping Matt Viviano shower would leave it in permanent shreds.

"Left. And right. Left, and right." They stepped the cadence into the small bathroom with Matt's arm draped around her shoulders.

"Sorry. I know I'm heavy."

"To say the least. But you're not leaning much."

"I'm trying not to. I'm real glad there's a little tile shelf I can sit on in that shower." He walked straight into it, still wearing his sweats. Larissa could see an outline of him through the shower doors as he lowered himself to the seat. The door opened a crack and his clothes came out. "Nuts."

"Now what?" It was strange standing there holding his clothing, still warm from his body and knowing that he was there a foot away without his clothes.

"I can't reach the water."

"How warm do you want it?"

"Warmer than body temperature. Not hot enough to boil lobsters."

"Okay." She slid the front half of the shower doors open far enough to put an arm inside and turn on the water. It was so tempting to just turn around and look. Even with surgical tape across his flanks, she knew Matt would be a treat. But she knew he wasn't supposed to be doing any quick moves, and if she turned around, he'd have to strangle her. So she was good. For the present. Holding her hand under the spray she felt it, then adjusted it.

"You have pretty arms."

"Thank you. I'm going to get you clean clothes. Holler if you need anything else."

She was trying to decide which drawer probably held his underwear when the shout came. Sprinting back to the shower she flung it open. He was still sitting on the tile shelf, dripping and grinning.

"Well, you said to holler. I needed the shampoo."

She nearly slammed the door in his face. "I think we're getting better."

"Slowly, Larissa. Slowly." Even in the steam that surrounded him she could see him grin.

"Not nearly fast enough." She handed him the shampoo and escaped.

Chapter Nine

"Wasn't it nice of Jory's little friend to ask him to go to the zoo?" Larissa said through gritted teeth.

"Just dandy." Matt looked up at the ceiling. "Think we could call and ask him to come back?"

"Not on a bet, Viviano. This is one less person for me to chase after for a few hours and I'm taking the opportunity. Besides, Jory was getting stir-crazy anyway. It was sweet of Scott's mother to ask him over."

"Right. She didn't know about our little problem."

That was putting it mildly. It *had* been kind of Scott's mother to ask Jory over. She had seen her action as taking a burden off someone just hours out of surgery, Larissa was sure. Not the removal of the only chaperone two crazy people had.

She had to be crazy by now. And surely Matt was. It was the only explanation for the attraction that had done much more than blossom in the last six hours. It had bloomed into an entire forbidden garden.

"Are you feeling any different?" Larissa asked cautiously.

"Not really. You?" Matt still wouldn't look anywhere but the ceiling.

Perhaps it had been his light-headedness when he came out of the shower that had triggered everything. It had certainly put them together physically. Larissa never knew that damp sweats could be so appealing.

For her it had been helping him towel off his hair. The heavy dark mass was almost curly when it was half wet. Smooth and silky through her fingers, it had a life of its own. She had never meant to stroke his cheek like that when she was drying his hair.

But it had happened. And since that one small moment, being in the same room together had been torture. They'd struggled through lunch and afterward Larissa had stretched out for just a moment far on the other side of Matt's bed. She was too tired to do anything else.

Coming awake two hours later with that heavy arm draped over hers was an electrifying experience. Matt's hazel eyes were even more intense than usual coming out of sleep. And his fingers trailing from her earlobe to the base of her throat nearly undid her. Larissa knew that taking a nap would not be a simple experience again until she forgot waking up from this one, and that would be months. Maybe years.

Naturally, when the invitation from Scott arrived, Jory was gone in record time. At first Larissa tried staying just far enough from Matt's room so that she could hear him but not see him.

It didn't work. Each strange little noise convinced her that her patient was probably doing something insane that would undo all his healing.

When she came back into the room she was certain she was right. "You got up, didn't you?" Matt's face against the pillows was a pale shade she hadn't thought was possible under his year-round tan.

"I forgot."

"That you're not supposed to get up? That should be pretty easy."

"No, not that part. Getting up all by itself is okay by now. Honest," he added when faced with her skeptical glare. "It was the book."

"The book?"

"Yeah. I hadn't realized how heavy that regulations notebook I'm updating was."

"And you picked it up and brought it over here, didn't you? Let's see that incision."

It wasn't pulled, not much. At least that was what Matt protested as she bullied him into seeing his stomach. The farther south past his navel the waistband of his sweats went, the less sure Larissa was that she was cut out for this nursing stuff. She was not thinking about seepage anymore when they came to the twin lines low on his belly.

"Right one looks okay. You pulled that left one pretty good, I think," she said, fingers skirting the tape that covered the incision. Most of the angry redness had disappeared from his skin. Between the incisions a trail of dark hair was crisp when her fingers brushed it, and unnerving. "I think you're okay. Want something for pain?"

"Yes. No." Matt ground back into his pillows with a growl. "I don't know. I just want something to distract me."

"From the pain or from me?"

"Both." He captured her wrist when she finished arranging his waistband and moving a sheet over him. When he brought her hand higher and nuzzled her palm Larissa gasped. "You feel it too, don't you?"

"For the last few hours. And I bet we can't blame it on your pain medication this time any more successfully than we blamed the Chianti last time, Matt. It's magic whether you like it or not."

"I like the results. What I don't like is the thought that I can't handle this." He closed his eyes for a minute, sinking back into the mound of pillows. "And I think I'll take some of that pain medication we can't blame."

She got it for him and he swallowed it without complaint for a change. Larissa thought the strain of picking up the book must have been worse than he was willing to let on.

He settled back into his pillows. Matt's face was slightly drawn. Around his mouth there were little white lines where the skin was pulled taut. "Twenty minutes, at least, before that kicks in. Distract me, Larissa. Tell me a story."

"Never thought I'd hear you say that. You don't like my stories, remember?"

"Now there's where you're wrong. I like them too much."

"But you still want one?"

His answering look was that of a tiger. "Left to our own devices, what else could we do until my pain pills kick in?"

She moved away from his supine form. "I get your drift." Settling onto the far side of the bed, she leaned against the headboard. This was going to be a challenge.

"You don't want Jory's story, right?"

"Correct. That one bothers me. Tell me something else. Heck, make one up."

Larissa took a deep breath, thinking. He'd become more precious to her than she wanted. Somehow recuperation from surgery hadn't dulled any of Matt's power to entrance her. If anything, it made him more dangerous.

This wasn't the way things were supposed to be happening. She had already given notice, begun to ease Matt Viviano out of her life. In a few short weeks she would be gone from here. It was ridiculous to be settled into this man's bed telling him stories.

She had to break this spell between them, get them through this swamp of feelings they were both mired in and onto firm ground on the other side. There were several ways she could think of to do that. But only one would work for sure. Once Matt heard this story she wouldn't have to worry anymore about his wanting another one.

Taking a deep breath, she began. "Once upon a time, down in the bootheel, there was a girl. Just an ordinary girl, no magic or anything. No fairy godmothers had blessed her and she wasn't any princess in disguise. Which is why she was so surprised when one day this handsome knight rode up on a white horse and offered to sweep her away."

"Ah, she should watch out," Matt said, slightly drowsy and still with closed eyes. "Those knights on white horses aren't always what they seem."

"I wish you had been down there with the girl," Larissa said. "Because you're sure right about this knight guy. He was handsome and had courtly manners. In no time at all he had wound himself around the girl's heart."

"And her bank account, too, I'll bet. Shining armor is expensive."

Larissa wondered how she was going to keep telling this story past the lump in her throat. "And her bank account, too. Matt, you are a veritable magician."

He must have heard the tears that had collected unshed. Matt's eyes flew open and his hand shot out to wind fingers around her. "Aw, Larissa, this is true, isn't it? This isn't something you're just weaving to keep me distracted."

She could only nod her head.

"Do you want to keep on? Because I want to keep listening."

"You may not later."

"If I want you to stop, I'll stop you."

He didn't stop her. But Matt began to look annoyed by the time she got to the part about the engagement with the ring that turned out to be glass. And by the time she'd gotten to the part about the joint bank accounts where money apparently flowed only one way, he looked almost livid. And when she finished up with the disappearance of not only the knight, but most of her worldly goods one fine day in May while she was at school, all he did was sputter for a while as he strangled a spare pillow with one hand.

"I felt so... ignorant," she said, looking up at the ceiling now herself, Matt's free hand still grasping hers. "Here I was, supposedly planning a wedding in three weeks, and abandoned nearly at the altar."

"Count yourself lucky. This guy was slime," he said finally through gritted teeth.

"Yeah, I figured that part out. But it sure has made me look twice at every decision I make. Now you know why I've been so grateful for payday." Larissa looked away from him, trying to absorb herself in the pattern of the wallpaper. "I couldn't have you looking at me like you were earlier and not know this."

"Know what? That you ran into a con artist?"

"No, that I fell for what he was selling."

It was so quiet in the bedroom. Behind her Larissa could hear heavy breathing, but she couldn't will herself to turn around and face the disappointment she heard in Matt's voice. "I know. It was pure, plain stupidity. Just call me a gal from the sticks, I guess. I'd been surrounded by good people all my life. It didn't occur to me to think that he wasn't what he seemed."

She didn't expect the gentle caress of her shoulders. "That's still the beauty of you, Larissa. That you can keep that innocence. Don't let one consummate jerk ruin it for you."

She turned, slowly. The disappointment just wasn't there. Matt's clear hazel eyes still held the soft feelings she had wanted to do away with. "Then you don't think I was stupid?"

"Naïve perhaps. But not stupid. Never that." He traced the pattern of the one lone tear she let escape. "If this story was meant to convince me of that somehow, you failed."

She couldn't quite smile yet. "No, I don't think I failed. In the oddest sort of way I feel more successful than I have in months."

They were close enough to kiss then, and Matt moved in closer. His warm lips reassured her that there was more success to come.

He hadn't put anything on besides sweatpants after his shower. Larissa's hands ran over his skin, feeling the warm satin of it, the bunched muscles underneath. He still smelled of bath soap and shampoo, with a current of male hunger underneath.

It was hard to hold her body away from his. But Larissa didn't want to press up against any spots that would cause him pain. She let Matt do all the moving even though it drove her mad to stay still.

The insistent pressure of his lips made the room spin. His tongue had edged in to tangle with hers in a dance that seduced the rest of her body into movement. The whimper that came from deep in her chest surprised her.

"I have to move. But I don't want to hurt you."

"That's supposed to be my line," Matt said.

"Not when you're the one with two healing incisions."

"For now just tell yourself that if it has cloth on it, it's off-limits."

"Okay." Larissa stared into his eyes, seeing the flames fan and ignite as she ran her hands down his sides just to the low-slung waist of his sweats and then back up to his chest. As she stroked gently his nipples hardened to match hers.

He found the buttons on her soft knit shirt. "This thing has got to go." And then in a moment it was gone. She expected him to make some comment about the undershirt she had on underneath. It felt girlish to her, not the attire of a woman who was being seduced. But then she had little experience with that.

Larissa had a feeling that even if she'd been under the scrutiny of a man's eyes a thousand times before that this would have felt new. Nothing could be the same as Matt's looking at her this way, a tentative finger tracing the pink ribbon that threaded through the neckline of her undershirt.

His mouth went down the path his finger had traced until she felt his hot breath on the blunt point of her breast. His mouth through the thin fabric created a sensation that lifted her off the bed.

At her cry of pleasure his head came up. When their gazes met, Matt went from passion to shock in a breath. "This is all very new to you, isn't it?"

"I'm afraid so." It was the first time Larissa had ever felt embarrassed about admitting her lack of experience. His look of regret said it all.

"Then we have to stop, Larissa."

"Why? Maybe once we get past this, we won't feel this way anymore. Maybe we can just relate to each other like anybody else."

The green flecks in his eyes flashed as she stared into them. "Do you really believe that?"

She couldn't hold his gaze any longer. "No."

"Neither do I. There would be more than once, Larissa. Infinitely more than once. And I can't break your heart like that." He seemed to draw into himself as he moved away.

"What do you mean?" she asked.

He was back to looking at the ceiling. "It wouldn't make any difference. This isn't forever. There won't be any more forevers for me, because just like your knights in armor, they don't last. We would make love. And it would be wonderful. But you would still go when your notice is up, Larissa. That's all there is for us."

The ceiling wasn't all that interesting, even when they were both looking at it. Larissa felt around for her shirt, wondering how women of the world handled situations this embarrassing. She was sure a woman of the world would have done better than bouncing off the bed and standing in the doorway struggling with the knit garment and a bushel basket full of hurt feelings.

"If that's the case, I need to make a phone call. To your mother. I'm giving you back to her while I go stay with Tess."

"Does this mean you're backing off on giving three weeks' notice?"

Larissa struggled to keep her voice calmer than she felt. "Oh, no. I'll be back Monday. But only for the rest of October. And only as the housekeeper, Matt. I can't handle what's going on with us anymore."

Matt didn't try to get up and cause any commotion after that. He knew that he should have gone after Larissa, tried to calm her down. But in the course of that calming down he would have probably made promises he had no intention of keeping. It was better this way, he told himself.

Connie was there before dark, bearing a casserole, as if she'd expected this all along. Matt could hear her and Larissa talking in the hall. Then there was some stirring downstairs and doors opening and closing and he knew Larissa was gone. There was a kind of electricity that left the house when she did. He hated to admit that he could tell the difference. The admission smacked too much of believing in the magic she wove.

But still it was there. When Larissa was here the house hummed to itself in happiness. When she left, the quiet was more quiet. He waited for his mother to climb the stairs again, hoping she'd bring him a pitcher of water and sit quietly by the bed. Laid out on the hassock were the vests Larissa had finished, waiting for buttons to be sewn on. Perhaps his mother would do that.

When Connie came into the room, Matt knew better. She wasn't going to leave him alone. She had the same look on her face she'd had when she'd found the dents on his dad's new car when he was seventeen. No rest for the wicked, at least not this evening.

For a while playing possum worked. Connie just sat by the bed while he kept his eyes closed and stayed very still. He was much too keyed up to sleep, so that didn't work long. Larissa had been right. He was like a cat on hot ashes. Once he gave up the pretense and sat up, his mother was ready for battle.

"You're making a major mistake here, Matt. Bigger than you know."

"Give it up, Mom. It's not going to work. I can't lead Larissa on. She's too good for that."

Connie's expression was probably a mirror of his own. Matt knew where he got his stubbornness from. It was evident in her sparkling eyes and firm jaw. "So don't lead her on. Do something else. Like marry the woman."

"No way, Mom. Never again." There was no comfortable spot on the bed. Finally he gave up trying to get comfortable and got up. He could pace, if he did it slowly. Besides, it would give his mother something else to worry about.

Unfortunately, even watching him pace didn't distract her. She did stand and come closer, but she was still on the same subject. "Give me one good reason you're going to let this woman walk out of your life, Matthew."

"Deanna."

"Give me a better reason."

Matt stopped where he was. "How can you say that? You know what I went through, what Jory went through. He didn't sleep for more than an hour or two for months, Mom. He spent most of the time from his second birthday to his third looking for someone who wasn't coming back."

"Mainly because he wasn't allowed to do anything else." She wasn't quite tall enough to take him by the shoulders and shake him. It was a shock to Matt to realize that his mother must be shrinking. That or maybe she'd always been this short. He'd just seen her as an indomitable force, not as a slightly tired looking woman in her early sixties. "Sit down, Matthew. We need to talk."

They ended up at the kitchen table. It was his first foray past the bedroom and once Matt got settled in a chair he felt comfortable. His mother's strong coffee and the inevitable plate of cookies were a comfort. Her words weren't.

"I thought I was doing the right thing. We all did." Her fingers around the mug she was cradling seemed to tremble a little. "We just sheltered you too long, Matthew."

Matt wanted to reach out, to stop her, but he had to hear what she was saying.

"Losing Deanna was a terrible thing. It was unexpected and awful. Only after everything was over did I realize you'd never even had to deal with death before. I guess our first mistake was keeping all you kids at home when we buried Nonna, wasn't it?"

"I wouldn't call it a mistake. Nobody thought much about it in those days. But yes, it would have been easier to deal with everything with Dee, maybe."

Connie shrugged. "And maybe not. There's no good way of dealing with losing a beautiful young woman in perfect health. But Matt, she's gone. She's been gone for over five years. And no amount of anger or worry will bring her back."

"I know that, Mom."

"Then why won't you live? And let your son live." Her eyes were sparkling with tears now. "Things happen, Matt. If you keep Jory boxed in where you always know exactly what he's doing, where he's going, then what happened to Dee is guaranteed not to happen to him. That's true. But Matt, he's the kind of active, intelligent little boy you were at that age. Can you imagine what would have happened if you had been closed in like this?"

"Where did I ever go?" The coffee was bitter on his tongue when he took a swallow.

"Everywhere. Don't you remember all the tadpoles you brought home? And the trips to the library? And what about Uncle Tadeo?"

"God, I'd forgotten about him."

"How can you possibly forget an old reprobate like him? If we hadn't let you wander by yourself, how would your best friend have been a seventy-two-year-old who made his own wine and taught you to tie flies?''

"We caught a lot of fish."

"And so should Jory. Or lightning bugs, or whatever it is he wants to catch, Matthew. And he should be doing it with Larissa. And so should you."

"You're probably right, Mom. But she's gone. And she's not coming back."

"Nonsense. She'll be back Monday."

"Her body will be back. But not her spirit, Mom. I just don't have the guts to keep that part here anymore. Besides, she's already given notice. After Halloween all of her will be gone."

Connie got up and went to the coffeepot to get them both another cup of coffee. "And if you let that happen you're a bigger fool than I ever thought possible."

"We'll see, Mom. We'll just have to see." Right now all Matt could see was the trouble he was going to have getting back up the stairs to bed.

Larissa's room felt like strange territory when she came back Monday morning. She could hear Matt at the other end of the hallway, but she didn't open the door to look. No, the farther away she stayed, the better.

Looking for a new place Sunday afternoon had been depressing. Everyone wanted too much money for awful little spaces. She wouldn't get anything like what she had here. None of the apartments she looked at had the big windows and even bigger closets of this old house.

The floors didn't creak companionably in the new places. And there wouldn't be any marvelous nooks to read a book in. But worst of all, no little boys would fling their arms around her neck first thing in the morning while she poured them both cereal. And no tall, brown-haired men would be waiting while she made coffee.

No, none of the places were right at all. Tess had told her about one of the other librarians who was looking for a housemate. Maybe she'd call her today on her break. It wouldn't be perfect, but it would be someplace to go.

And she needed someplace to go. It was going to be murder keeping up the pretense of just being the housekeeper. Pretending that every little noise from that room down the hall didn't want to send her knocking on the door. Pretending that it wasn't the best part of her day when she got to tuck Jory in.

Sighing, she gathered up her tote bag and went to pack a lunch for school. Connie and Jory were both in the kitchen when she got there. "I already made you a sandwich, when I made Jory's," Connie told her, brandishing a paper bag. "And I put a few other things in there too. You look like somebody who could use a nutritious lunch."

Jory was by her side at the kitchen counter. "I'm short on hugs. I didn't get any yesterday, not from you."

She bent down and gathered him in her arms. It wasn't what her mind told her to do. The more practical part of her was already whispering that she should be weaning him away from her so that when she left, it wouldn't be terrible.

But her heart knew differently. All the rationality in the world wasn't going to prepare either of them for her leaving. It would be terrible no matter what. So for now Larissa filled her arms with a little boy who smelled of sunshine and cinnamon and wondered how she had ever lived without him. Or how she would live without him again in a few short weeks. She was never going to survive.

Chapter Ten

It was two weeks of living hell. Larissa had no other description for the time from mid-October to Halloween. Going to work every day, coming home and ignoring Matt while she fixed dinner, then eating with him and Jory with as little personal conversation as possible. Since Matt was still off from work recuperating, Jory spent the evening with him until bedtime. But he still insisted on being tucked in by both of them.

Matt looked healthier every day. By the end of the first week he had taken over cooking dinner. It was fascinating coming home to the smell of garlic and basil and other tempting things every afternoon. Watching him stand over the stove stirring something with a wooden spoon was a sight Larissa knew she could have come home to every day of her life. Especially if he kept wearing those low-slung jeans and soft sweaters he favored when he wasn't in his work uniform.

She got used to talking to the back of him while he cooked. "I won't be moving until the third of November," she told that tempting back view while she sat at the kitchen table. For a moment the set of his shoulders looked almost relieved. Then he straightened and turned to face her and she could see he was as nonchalant as she wished she felt.

"Oh? Plans get hung up?"

"Just a little. My new housemate wants to wait until the weekend. We can use her van then anyway to move all my books."

"Poor woman will never know what hit her."

Why did his smile have to be so enchanting? Larissa finished the last of her after-school snack. She couldn't even fault him on that part of the housekeeping he'd taken over. His oatmeal cookies were wonderful. She wasn't about to let on that she suspected they came from the store in the mall where he was walking in the mornings to build up his endurance.

"Why are you still paying me, Viviano? You're doing the cooking, taking care of Jory after school, the whole nine yards." She tossed her used napkin into the trash.

"I'm paying you because you're still my housekeeper. You still take Jory to school and pick him up when he isn't on the bus. And you are still doing the cleaning and the laundry."

"Only because you can't lift the baskets." It felt good to talk to him, even if they were arguing. Larissa wanted to tell him how much she missed him. She wanted to walk into his arms instead of out of his life.

But that wasn't going to happen and she needed to work on next year's budget.

"If you'd rather I didn't pay you I can arrange that. I'll be out of your hair next week anyway. For a couple of days you're going to have to earn that paycheck before you move."

"Got your doctor's appointment set up?"

"Monday at two. And by then I'll be able to drive myself. In fact, I expect him to release me to go back to work immediately."

"But you'll wait until the first of November, right? I mean, two in the afternoon is a little late in the day to start."

He still had that little half dimple when he grinned. Larissa wanted to strangle him for remaining so attractive when she was trying to convince herself he was an ogre and a fiend.

"Right. Maybe we can go out to dinner that night to celebrate."

"Maybe we can't. It's Halloween, remember? Even if you don't let your child go out, there will be dozens of little ghouls from the neighborhood ringing the doorbell. And heaven help you if your lights are off and it looks uninhabited."

"My lights are always off after dark and it always looks haunted around here. What makes you think they'll bother us that night?"

"I told you, it's Halloween. Besides, I have to pack then anyway."

He huffed in aggravation, standing too close for Larissa to be comfortable. "You don't have that many books. If you're not moving until the weekend, put it off a little, can't you?"

"I'm not just packing for that. The school district is sending me to a seminar in St. Louis on storytelling. I get to tell some and listen to some for three days starting the first. But don't worry, I'll be done in time to meet the school bus every afternoon."

"Fine. No dinner out. No company. And I get to answer the door for a couple dozen little monsters. My idea of a perfect evening."

Even stalking off he looked all too good. Larissa shook her head. It was going to be a long weekend, even if it was only two days.

Matt stood in the driveway waiting for the school bus. He could hardly wait for Jory to get off so that he could tell somebody the good news about his doctor's appointment. He'd rather it was Larissa, but his son would do just fine. Especially since subtlety was failing to work on Larissa.

And she had called *him* stubborn. She was really sticking to her guns on this. If he wanted her back, he was going to have to agree to all kinds of things he couldn't see doing, like long-term commitment with marriage as part of the package.

There were times like now, standing in the fall sunshine listening to the birds, when it sounded like a good idea. They were compatible in almost every way. Jory liked her. And neither of them would ever lack for excitement with Larissa around. Besides, if she agreed to stay he could stop going broke buying those cookies at the mall.

But in the end nothing had changed. If he was married to Larissa, he would want her meeting the school bus instead of him, even on a day like this. Each little note like the one she'd left him this morning telling him she would be working late would strike fear in his heart.

He could hear the grinding gears of the bus as it lumbered around the corner. It stopped two houses down and three figures got off. One was a tiny fairy princess with gold wings. One was a makeshift ghost who looked as if he'd raided his mother's linen closet. The third was a clown with neon hair. Jory wasn't one of them.

The driver stopped for Matt's frantic wave.

"Where's Jory?"

"He didn't get on the bus. I figured he was coming home with Ms. Camden."

"He wasn't. He was supposed to be on the bus."

The driver shrugged. "Well, he didn't get on." She turned and polled the remaining children on the bus. No one had seen him since class let out. "Call the school," she suggested, and vanished in a cloud of dirt kicked up from the road.

Matt didn't like the way his heart was beating. Jory wasn't on the bus, and he was pretty sure that Larissa was still at school. Perhaps she'd let Jory stay after with her. That was it. He went inside, grabbed his keys and wallet and was in the truck in a flash. The mile and a half to school passed quickly. When he got there, the parking lot was suspiciously empty. Even most of the faculty lot was bare.

The front doors were still unlocked and he went in, hoping he could find his way to the library. All the way there, he imagined his relief when he saw the small figure who would be hanging on to Larissa's chair while she worked, telling her one of his endless stories.

Except the library was dark when he got there. In the back a little light shone through under the door to the office. He walked through the dim space, conscious of the smells of new paper and cleaning supplies. Then he opened the door.

Larissa faced away from him, busy at a computer terminal. And she was alone.

"Where's Jory?"

"Should be three quarters of the way home by now, at least. I reminded him this morning to take the bus."

Matt felt sweat break out on his body. "Well, he didn't get on it."

She turned to face him, forehead wrinkled in consternation. "Now, that just isn't like him to forget. No, wait. He would have come here if he had forgotten. Let's go to the office."

The office staff was polite but firm. No one had come in to report missing a bus, especially not any first graders. Jory's teacher was already gone for the day, but a call to the Clemens household let them know that he'd left the classroom with everyone else and hadn't come back.

Larissa hung up the phone and turned to Matt. "No luck. Let me go back to my office and turn off the computer. We'll start looking."

"We should call the police," Matt said. He was shaking slightly. Larissa came to him and put her hands on his shoulders. Underneath her fingers his body was tense.

"He's just fooling around, Matt. Everything's okay." She tried to sound confident, but it was hard. She didn't feel very confident anymore. Matt's fear was contagious.

He tore himself away from her. "Everything is *not* okay. My son is missing."

"Okay. Calm down enough to look for him. It won't help to get this upset, you won't think clearly. And let's not call the police just yet, okay? They won't do anything this early anyway."

"I know." There was too much knowledge in Matt's eyes. "This is all like a nightmare."

"Well, we're going to get you awake soon. Follow me to the office."

She turned off the computer and left a note on the door for Jory in case they had missed each other somehow. In her heart, Larissa knew that note would still be there the next time she checked. She didn't like to admit it, but Matt's panic was catching.

"Okay, let's start. We'll both drive home. You take the direct route and I'll take the way we go if we're going to have ice cream after school. It's a three block detour. If he decided to walk home, he'd go one of those two ways. We'll meet back at the house and if neither of us has him then, we'll go from there."

Matt nodded. He looked as if he were on automatic pilot. Larissa had never seen him this way, not even right after his surgery.

Half an hour in the car combing the neighborhood didn't do anything for his disposition. When she pulled into the driveway he was sitting on the front porch, head down, hands tangled in his disordered dark hair.

"We've got to find him. God, Larissa, what if he's in a ditch somewhere, or somebody snatched him from school?"

She sat down beside him and put her arm around him. It was the only thing she could do and it was nowhere near enough to reassure him. "We'll find him. And it won't be in a ditch and it won't be because somebody has snatched him," she said firmly. "Let's sit out here in case he walks up. I'll get the phone book and the portable phone and we'll start making calls."

When an hour had passed and there was still no Jory, Matt called the police, and then his mother. Larissa held his hand while he made the calls. His voice nearly broke when he told Connie what was going on. "Yes, we called the police. They said they'd send someone over by six if we still wanted an officer. Yes, I know that's after dark. God, Mother, what am I going to do?"

He pushed the button on the handset that hung up the phone. "She's coming over. I don't know what she'll do, but I think it will help."

"It sure will. We'll let her stay here in case anybody calls or comes and we're going other places." Larissa squeezed his hand. "Let's go up to Jory's room."

Nothing seemed out of place or missing. The bag he'd put his Halloween costume in was gone, but Larissa knew he had taken it with him to school for Mrs. Clemens's costume party. All his other clothes were in order. "Well, we know he didn't run away."

"Or if he did, he didn't pack anything."

Larissa shook her head. "He's not quite seven years old, Matt. And he'd take this seriously. If he was going to run away, his pajamas would be gone, and Flat Cat. And the book he's been reading. He's only on Chapter Six." It was hard to keep her voice from trembling. "No, he hasn't run away. He had a normal school day. None of his classmates that we could reach noticed anything odd."

"But none of them were with him when he left school, either. Should we try again at Scott's house?"

"Nobody will be home there until six," Larissa said. "His folks both work and he goes to day care. I'll call Mary again and find out which one."

Two calls later Larissa didn't feel as if she had any new information. A quick check with Scott at day care yielded no more new information, except that he and Jory had talked about trick-or-treating during lunch. Scott had even told him the two jokes he was going to use when he rang doorbells. But Jory had walked out of school just like normal before vanishing into thin air.

Larissa was more worried about Matt, even now, than she was about Jory. He was a shade of gray that human skin shouldn't take on. "We're going to find him, Matt. I know we will. It's all some kind of silly mistake we just haven't figured out yet."

His eyes were haunted. "I don't think so. He's gone."

"People don't just vanish like that," Larissa said. Except they did. How often had she picked up her newspaper to read of just that, usually small children? But that couldn't happen to Jory.

"They do. I know that, firsthand."

The hair on the back of her neck stood up. "Does this have to do with your wife in some way? If so, you better tell me about it so I know how to handle all this."

He took a deep, ragged breath. "She said she was going to school. Except she never got there."

"She was a teacher?"

Matt shook his head, looking down into the grass. "Student. Once Jory was born she decided to go back for a master's degree so that once we'd had our family and everything she could be a social worker. I came home that night like always, kissed her goodbye, and she drove off. I put the baby to bed, did some stuff around the house, and started wondering when it was ten o'clock and she still wasn't home."

His face was hard now, reliving it all. "The police found her car by the side of the highway with a flat tire. She knew better than to get out, but she was only about a quarter mile from an exit and Dee was always an optimist.

"It was spring and it would have been getting dark when she left the car. At first they figured maybe somebody grabbed her. They started searching, but nothing turned up. Three days later some kids poking around in a creek near the highway found her."

"Had she been murdered?"

His laugh held no humor. "Now that's the ironic part. They figure a truck hit her and she went down an embankment into the creek. It wasn't murder in the usual sense. But it took my wife, and Jory's mother. And my confidence that the world is a good place to live. Because there were probably a dozen people who saw all that happen, including a truck driver who had to have known he hit something. And no one ever said a word."

Larissa looked down, realizing she'd been holding his hand so tightly through his story that he probably had no circulation in his fingers. "It's light out. And everybody was excited at school, with the holiday and all. Nothing like that happened to Jory. We've got to find him. I know we can, together."

Larissa was so keyed up by the events of the afternoon and Matt's revelation that there was a buzzing in her head. She lay back gently on the porch with Matt looking at her, questioning.

"I got a little light-headed. But I'll be okay. I have to be. I've got to help you find him." There was something nudging her. Those words seemed important. More important, there was something real and physical poking her in the back. She shifted around to see what she had squashed. It was Jory's Flat Cat. When they'd left his room, Matt had absently brought it with him and put it down on the porch while they'd made their fruitless series of calls.

She could see Jory holding it. Jory, up in her lap as much as somebody that long legged and bony could be. Jory, with tear-stained face telling her she had to stay. "Because when I get lost, he won't be able to find me." Not *if*. *When*.

Suddenly first grade logic became very clear. Larissa sat straight up. "I have to check something." She went into the house and up the stairs. Things were just the way she now expected them to be. Going down the stairs she went so fast she nearly missed the last step. Matt looked startled when the screen door banged. "We have to get back in the truck."

"Why?"

"I can't explain. I just think I know where he is. Or at least why he is wherever he is. How long will it take your mom to get out here?"

"With rush hour traffic? Another fifteen minutes at least."

"Good. Let's call Scott again."

Matt looked very confused, but he complied. If he understood any of Larissa's questions to the boy, he didn't show it. But when Connie pulled up in the driveway he dutifully got into his truck and let Larissa take the passenger seat as she directed him into a neighborhood four miles away.

"Now remember, no yelling. None at all until after we get back to the house and he's had a bath and supper and everything. Crying is okay, hugging is okay, but no yelling."

"No yelling. It may blow my incisions not to, but I promise, Larissa, if we find him like you say we're going to, no yelling."

Larissa strained to see in the growing twilight. Relief washed over her in a wave, and she fought not to sob. "Turn onto that court. Oh. Oh, my. Stop the truck."

Matt was stopped and out in a flash. They could see the small figure coming toward them, dragging a pillowcase. When it got closer, under a street light that had just turned on, there was Jory in his coonskin cap. "It was nearly full. And I was going to come home when it got dark. But I kinda got lost."

"So you should have told somebody."

"That I got lost trick-or-treating? Then they would know for sure that I wasn't from this neighborhood. They might have taken my candy."

"I'm going to beat them to it," Matt said. Larissa wasn't sure if he was trying to get down on Jory's level or if his knees collapsed. Whatever the result, he knelt on the sidewalk and took the bag away from his son. "Let's go home, Jordan."

"Okay." He didn't argue, in fact he seemed relieved to be found and taken home. He submitted to his father's long hug, and then they all three got into the truck. There was no talking in the truck until they got to the driveway.

"Grandma's inside. And when she sees you she's probably going to cry," Matt told his son. "We were all very worried."

They went inside. Grandma, as predicted, cried. And after giving a wide-eyed Jory a giant hug and a little shake, she went into the kitchen because, she said, "everyone will be hungry once we get over this." Matt sent Jory upstairs to take a shower and put his pajamas on before anyone ate. Once they heard the bathroom door close, Larissa reflexively turned to Matt and hugged him, as hard as Connie had hugged Jory. She let him shudder out the few tears he allowed himself in her arms.

"God, I was so scared. But we found him. No—*you* found him."

"He knew I would. I don't know whether to hug him or hurt him for that." Larissa wiped away the tears she, too, had held in until Jory was safe. "Now go help him dry off and get some food into him before you ground him for life, okay?"

Matt was wet-eyed, but more put together than she'd seen him all day. "Sure. You joining us?"

She shook her head. "I still have to pack. For my seminar, remember? I've got books and papers galore that need to be organized before I go."

She stood at the foot of the stairs for a moment, turning to face Matt, who was still in the middle of the hallway. "I think this is where we say goodbye. Our real goodbyes, Matthew. I know it's still a few days before I was supposed to leave. But tonight told me so many things about you." She swallowed hard. This was more difficult than she had expected.

"I love you, more than anyone else I've ever known. It would be like heaven on earth to stay here with you and Jory, to marry you and have more little Vivianos to make this house the loud kind of place it ought to be. Knowing what I know now about you, seeing you while we looked for him, I can't ask you to do that. You're just not ready. Maybe you never will be."

"Maybe you're right," he agreed gravely.

She went up two stairs. "If you decide you're ready, tell me. Loud and clear so I don't have any doubts. Because until you do, I'll go on loving you and Jory forever. But not here under this roof. That would tear my heart out." And then she was gone up the stairs and closed her door.

She stared at it from her side most of the night, waiting for a knock that didn't come. The only person staring at it harder was the man on the other side who couldn't bring himself to take the first step.

Chapter Eleven

Tuesday morning Matt woke up early. It hadn't been a restful night's sleep. He'd been thinking too much about what Larissa had said. Every time he'd startled awake during the night from one bad dream or another, he'd rehearsed his arguments on why things wouldn't work between them. Why he couldn't possibly let her into his life. Why a marriage between the two of them would be a disaster.

There was only one thing wrong with all his arguments. In the cold light of day once he'd gotten out of bed, none of them had much strength. In the middle of the night in the dark he could still convince himself that he was meant to be single for the rest of his life. That it would be cruel to Larissa to subject her to all his worries and fears if they did stay together.

In the morning it was better to wonder what would happen if they did take the fatal plunge and get married. What would it be like to have an awful nightmare and wake up next to Larissa? To twine his fingers in that pale hair and stroke her shoulder until she turned to him sleepily to ask what the matter was. And to know that she would gather him into her arms until the echoes of the nightmare passed. Perhaps they would even take advantage of both being awake in the middle of the night without any children around...

Matt stood at the window of his bedroom looking out at the woods behind the house. He'd have to build a treehouse out there. Jory needed to climb and jump and do all of the things he'd been too afraid to let him risk. He needed to go looking for frogs and find them, to do all the things Larissa had insisted were essential to a young man's development. And it would be pretty good if he could do them with a little brother or sister tagging along for company.

Matt had to admit this house had never been what he wanted it to be. They'd been in only a matter of months when Dee died. It was supposed to have been their dream retreat from the city; instead it had always been his cave where he'd spent years of being a hermit.

"No more," he said out loud. It was time to let the sunshine in all the windows. Maybe even hang some of those sparkly glass things he was sure Larissa would like. God, he'd spend his weekends going to craft fairs and storytelling festivals. Pushing a stroller eventually. He could hardly wait.

He pulled on jeans hurriedly and walked down the hall to her room. Three knocks and more, no one answered. He paused and listened for running water. Being in the shower was about the only excuse for not opening the door when someone was pounding on it this hard. No luck. It was silent inside.

She was in the kitchen having breakfast with Jory. Had to be. Matt hadn't intended to pour his heart out the first time in front of his son, but going down the stairs it didn't sound like such a terrible idea. After all, Jory had brought the two of them together by bringing Larissa home to dinner that first time. It was fitting that he witness this.

Except that when Matt got down to the kitchen Jory was the only one there.

"Oh, Larissa left a long time ago. Maybe half an hour," his son told him, looking up from a bowl of cold cereal. "She said she needed to get there early and the traffic would be nasty."

Jory stirred the last of the multicolored mess in his bowl, leaving a trail through the milk. "Do you think she felt okay, Dad? She looked like I feel when I have a stomach ache, but she said she wasn't sick."

It gave Matt hope, the first he'd felt since he came down to the kitchen. "I think she's going to be okay, Jory. But we're going to have to go get her."

"Why? She's at that story thing and I have to go to school."

It was a school day. And Matt had no idea how he would talk to Larissa once he had her face-to-face. Not in a hallway crowded with people at a seminar. He could never force the words out there, he knew. But he had to tell her how he felt and it had to be to-day before the sun set. That much he felt in his heart. He wasn't going to give Larissa any chance to move out and separate herself from them. She belonged here. Now that he was willing to admit that, he had to move fast.

He sat next to Jory and absentmindedly shook the box of cereal, listening to it rattle. As the two of them sat there, Matt began to get an idea. Larissa had told him to tell her loud and clear in language she couldn't miss that he was ready to be with her. He could think of one way that would tell her more clearly than any eloquent words. Larissa was the word person. He was mostly action, and it was time to take an unmistakable one.

"Hey, Jory, tell me how to call the school and tell them you're going to stay home today."

Jory's eyes got wide. "Am I in trouble that bad for last night?"

Matt laughed. "No. You're in trouble for last night, make no mistake. You may not stop being in trouble for last night until you're twelve, but after today you're going to school. Today I need you to help me convince Larissa to stay. For good."

"Okay. That's worth missing school." Jory told him where to find the instructions to call, and Matt did, leaving a message on the school's answering machine. Then he sat back down at the table with a wiggling Jory.

"Now tell me that story like Larissa tells it. And I'm going to ask a whole bunch of questions. I can start it out. 'Once way up in the mountains, in the hills of the Ozarks was a girl with an unusual name....'"

"Of course, everybody had strange names back then, like Jedidiah and Methuselah and Hepsibah," Jory picked up where he left off and for an hour Matt sat listening and questioning and planning his strategy.

* * *

It was a little stuffy in the seminar room. Or maybe Larissa was just a little nervous. There were ceiling fans and they were stirring up a breeze. It must be just the nerves from telling her story in front of this many people who really knew how to judge quality. It was one thing telling little kids. As long as it was a good story, well told, they were an appreciative audience. Heaven help you if you bored them, but otherwise they were fun.

This was different. Larissa felt like pacing instead of warming up to tell "Truelove" as usual. And if she was honest with herself, the audience was only part of the reason for her nerves. Some of it was because of what she'd left at home.

Home. She'd have to stop thinking of Matt's house that way. He hadn't gotten up and said anything this morning. And she'd never conquered her pride enough to go bang on his door until he let her in and they could settle things one way or another. If Matt had come to the door in the usual disreputable pair of gym shorts Larissa knew he slept in, there would have been only one resolution. But instead she had chickened out and left the house early.

So now here she was and there was someone introducing her. It was an honor to be picked as only one of four participants to do this, she told herself. She took a deep breath, then another, letting them out slowly to try to calm down to tell her story. It would be all right once she started telling it. She could get lost in the magic, even if she didn't believe all of it anymore.

It was hard to tell a story about a woman who faced unbelievable odds and still overcame them just to win a man when her man wouldn't cross the hallway to make things all right. More than that, she would never tell this story again without hearing Jory's voice piping up to tell it with her, seeing that dark blond head nodding, see those hazel eyes sparkling. This was Jory's story as much as it was hers now. In a strange sort of way she felt as if they were part of the same family because of it. But they'd never be family now, and the man in the front of the room was nearly done introducing her.

There was some applause and she got to the front of the room. "Thank y'all for coming this afternoon," she told them. There was a young man in the front row, maybe early twenties. He looked more alert than anyone else after their lunch break, and his sparkling eyes, although blue, reminded her of Jory and Matt's with their humor. She would tell the story to him. It wouldn't be the same, but she would have a focus that way.

First she gave her "professional" introduction, the one where she explained about Gilette and Italy and how the story had somehow made its way to the mountains in the heartland of America. Then she explained a little about how she'd found one version of the tale and changed this and that to make it hers. Now hers and Jory's, but she didn't tell the audience that.

Finally she pushed her hair back, and moved the sleeves of her soft turtleneck sweater so that they were just below her elbows. She needed her hands freed up to do this. Matt would laugh at her. He knew she couldn't talk without her hands moving. But now was certainly not the time to think about Matt. It was the time to think about her story. "Once way up in the mountains..." It was getting easier already.

They were an appreciative audience. Being story-tellers, or wanting to be, themselves, they oohed and aahed and nodded in the right places, laughing at Truelove's antics and almost booing Sally Lou Hutchins. Even when the door to the room opened and closed, admitting a latecomer, no one looked around. There was a scattering of applause when they got to the really good part and Sally Lou Hutchins got hers. By then Larissa had managed to shake off her melancholy and she was strutting up the street with Truelove, feeling triumphant.

"So she sashayed up the biggest street of that little bitty town," she told them all. "It wasn't a very long walk, but for Truelove it felt pretty long. She was scared, a little. There she was with everything Jeff told her she needed. She had his ring on her finger. It glimmered in the sunlight and Truelove figured it must be blinding anybody trying to peek out a window at her.

"And it couldn't be anybody's baby but Jeff's in her arms. The little one was the spit'n image of his father. Anybody could see that as he balanced on his mama's hip. And then, she was to the door of the general store. She took a deep breath and put her hand on the big brass knob."

Larissa always paused here for a bit of dramatics, taking a deep breath herself, squaring her shoulders, tossing her hair back from where it always fell over her face by now and looking up and back as if that big old oak door was in front of her.

Except this time something much more daunting was in front of her. No one else could see, nor would

they know the significance of what they saw even if
they did. Standing at the back of the room was a tall
man with wavy dark hair. He wore a hand-knitted
striped vest. And in his arms he held a child. The child
was a little big to be carried like this, but in the
crowded room it looked as if his father was just
holding him up for a view of the storyteller.

Larissa's pause took much longer than she intended. The hum of the ceiling fans was incredibly
loud in her ears, or maybe it was the pulsing of her
own heart. How would she go on from here knowing
Matt was watching her? She had to.

She took another deep breath. "Truelove took another deep breath and opened the door. There had
been a lot of noise and talking in the store like there
was any afternoon, but when everyone saw her
standing there it stopped. Even the old fellers playing checkers in the corner stopped. 'Well I swan,
Hiram,' the oldest one said, 'She's gone and done it.
Truelove done come back.'"

"So she walked over to the counter where Jeff was
measuring out dry goods. She walked up to him with
Little Jeff in her arms and his ring on her finger...."
And there in the back of the room stood Matt Viviano wearing the vest she had made him and carrying
Jory on his hip. Jory was dressed in his vest, too.
They couldn't have stood out more to her in that moment if they'd been bathed in light like a lighthouse.
Her gift on his back and their child in his arms. Matt
was saying it, here in front of everyone without saying a word.

"Go on," he mouthed silently. She must have
stopped still with her mouth hanging open. Damn,

where was she? People would start looking at her funny before long.

"His ring on her finger," Jory piped up. "And then she said..."

If people found it odd, they didn't say anything. About half the audience did turn toward Matt and Jory, but they looked back at Larissa when she went on. She was telling the story only for the two in the back of the room anyway now.

"And then she said, 'Well, here I am.' And Jeff, he smiled." Her own smile was tremulous and she just knew the tears were going to start running down her face any moment. "'There you are,' he said, 'with my ring on your finger and a youngun that can't be anybody's but mine in your arms. Why don't you put him down? He looks heavy.'"

That little detour was lost on everyone but Matt, who did let Jory slide to the ground beside him. Larissa was grateful because she knew his doctor would have kittens if he saw Matt lifting anything as heavy as Jordan right now, even for the best cause in the world. "So he took her in his arms and he kissed her." Larissa didn't remember moving to the middle of the room, but her feet had taken her there. She continued. "And he told her, 'Surely you're my own Truelove. And now I'll take you home.' So he locked the store and they went home. Where, due to an unforeseen circumstance, I have to go myself right now. Thank y'all for listening."

There was applause behind her as she pulled the two of them out the door and closed it behind her. "Tell me this means exactly what I think it does."

Matt leaned her against the wall, his strong arms around her. "How could it mean anything else?

You're the word person, Larissa. I do much better with actions." He kissed her, softly. "I guess I've got to use the words, too. I owe you that much."

There might have been other people in the hallway, but Larissa didn't notice as Matt looked down into her face, sheltering her with his broad body. "Larissa, I love you. And I'm scared silly right now, but I still want to marry you. Nothing would be worse than seeing you walk away just because I'm scared sometimes."

"We're all scared sometimes, Matt. But it's more comforting to be scared together."

"You said it. So, are we going home, really? Or do you need to do anything else here? I didn't mean to ruin your story."

She pulled him down and kissed him. "You didn't ruin it, not for the audience. I don't know if I can ever tell it again and not cry, but you didn't ruin it for them."

"You can't cry when you tell it, Larissa. It's a happy story," Jory told her. "And it's my story now. I thought it was before, but now I know it is. I even got to be Little Jeff, didn't I?"

"You sure did. And why don't you go back in there while they're taking their break and get my bag, okay? It's the one I take back and forth to school, with the alligators on it, and it's on the big desk in the front of the room."

"Okey-dokey," he said, going to the doorway.

Larissa didn't know whether to cry or holler or what. Instead she felt the most awful giggles well up and bubble forth while she watched Matt watch her and smile.

He pulled her in for a quick hug. "You going to be upset if anybody comes out of that door and sees me kissing you?"

She got the giggles under control. "I think we can risk it."

It was a jubilant kiss. A kiss that said things that words couldn't. "You were right about that one, Larissa. And I think we all need to take a few more risks. Like getting married. I'm willing to risk that one if you are."

His eyes fairly glowed as Larissa looked up at him. "Only if we do it real quick before I get scared."

He held up a hand. "Remember, we'll get scared together."

Jory came out, carrying Larissa's bag. "Who's scared? Those guys in there asked me if you two were getting married. I told them yes. Four of the people asked if they could watch. Is it okay if I told them yes?"

Matt groaned. "Okay, so maybe he doesn't need to take too many more risks."

"No, but we sure do. And if having a couple of cultural anthropologists at the wedding is the first new risk I take, so be it. Right now I want to go home."

Matt wrapped one arm around her, gathered the bag from Jory, and they started down the hall. "Great," Jory said. "When we get home will you tell me the story again? I want to make sure it doesn't make you cry. Besides, I only got to hear half of it this time."

Larissa reached across Matt and ruffled the boy's hair. "You'll hear all the story, Jordan. As long as you don't mind if I tell your dad one once you go to bed.''

The squeeze Matt gave her spoke volumes. Larissa didn't dare look up at him because she knew if she did, they'd have to explain to Jory what they were laughing about.

Jory continued to walk along, unconcerned. ''The story you tell him, Larissa. Will it have a happy ending?''

Larissa's laugh echoed through the halls of the building. ''Jory, your daddy is the happy ending to my story.''

''Oh.'' Jory looked puzzled for a minute, then his face brightened. ''Does that mean we're starting a new story now?''

Larissa nodded. ''A brand new one. How shall we start it?''

''Once upon a time there were three people who loved each other very much,'' Matt said.

Larissa looked into his face. ''For a man of few words, you manage to choose the right ones. Let's go home, Matt.''

And that's where they went. Home.

*　*　*　*　*

This July, watch for the delivery of...

An exciting new miniseries that appears in a different
Silhouette series each month. It's about love,
marriage—and Daddy's unexpected need for
a baby carriage!

Daddy Knows Last unites five of your favorite authors
as they weave five connected stories about baby
fever in New Hope, Texas.

- **THE BABY NOTION** by Dixie Browning
  (SD#1011, 7/96)

- **BABY IN A BASKET** by Helen R. Myers
  (SR#1169, 8/96)

- **MARRIED...WITH TWINS!**
  by Jennifer Mikels
  (SSE#1054, 9/96)

- **HOW TO HOOK A HUSBAND (AND A BABY)**
  by Carolyn Zane
  (YT#29, 10/96)

- **DISCOVERED: DADDY** by Marilyn Pappano
  (IM#746, 11/96)

Daddy Knows Last arrives in July...only from

MILLION DOLLAR SWEEPSTAKES
AND EXTRA BONUS PRIZE DRAWING

SWP-ME96

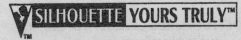

What do women really want to know?

Trust the world's largest publisher of
women's fiction to tell you.

HARLEQUIN ULTIMATE GUIDES™

I CAN FIX THAT

A Guide For Women
Who Want To Do It Themselves

This is the only guide a self-reliant
woman will ever need to deal
with those pesky items that
break, wear out or just don't work
anymore. Chock-full of friendly
advice and straightforward,
step-by-step solutions to the
trials of everyday life in our
gadget-oriented world! So, don't
just sit there wondering how to
fix the VCR—run to your
nearest bookstore for your copy now!

Available this May, at your favorite retail outlet.

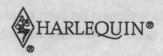

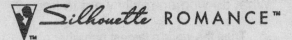
Silhouette ROMANCE™

is proud to present Carla Cassidy's
TWENTY-FIFTH book:

DADDY ON THE RUN
by
CARLA CASSIDY
(SR #1158, June)

Book four of her miniseries

Just when she was beginning to rebuild her life, Julianne Baker's
husband, Sam, was back! He had left only to protect her and their
little girl—but would Julianne be able to trust her husband's love
again, and give their family a second chance at happiness?

The Baker Brood: Four siblings in search of justice find love along
the way....

Don't miss the conclusion of **The Baker Brood** miniseries,
Daddy on the Run, available in June, only from

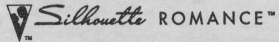
Silhouette ROMANCE™

Readers just can't seem to get enough of
New York Times bestselling author

Sandra Brown

This May, a mother searches for

A Secret Splendor

(previously published under the pseudonym Erin St. Claire)

Arden Gentry is searching for the son she was forced to give
up. But finding him could resurrect all the half-truths, secrets
and unspeakable lies that surrounded his birth. Because it
means finding the man who fathered her baby....

Find out how it all turns out, this May at your favorite
retail outlet.

 MIRA The brightest star in women's fiction